250

After al

want to

"Leslie, don't shut me out. I didn't mean to embarrass you. I know this is a tough situation. I just want to help any way I can. You know by now that I care."

That stopped Leslie in her tracks. Turning, she found his expression filled with compassion. Her heart skipped a beat when he placed his hands on her shoulders. She found that words wouldn't come.

"I don't want you to be afraid of how you're going to deal with all of this," Darrin said softly. "I just want you to know that I'm here for you."

"I know that," Leslie whispered. Her voice sounded foreign in her ears. "You've been a good friend, Darrin."

He pulled her into his arms and kissed her long and passionately. Leslie felt goosebumps travel down her spine. His lips were warm and gentle against hers, and for a moment, Leslie forgot who she was and why she was worried in the first place.

TRACIE PETERSON AND JENNIFER PETERSON have worked as a mother/daughter team for many years, but this is the first time they have plotted to write a book together. Jennifer loves to edit her mother's novels (over twenty **Heartsong Presents** titles), and Tracie says she has learned a lot from having Jennifer's input. They live in Topeka, Kansas, with the rest of the family: Jim, Julie, and Erik.

Crossroads

*Tracie Peterson and
Jennifer Peterson*

Heartsong Presents

A note from the Author:
I love to hear from my readers! You may correspond with me by writing:

Tracie Peterson and
Jennifer Peterson
Author Relations
P.O. Box 719
Uhrichsville, OH 44683

ISBN 1-57748-197-6

CROSSROADS

Cover illustration by John Monteleone.

PRINTED IN THE U.S.A.

one

"Hi, Daddy! How's Dallas?" Leslie Heyward cradled the cordless phone between her head and her shoulder as she stirred a pot of boiling spaghetti. "Oh, yeah, Travis is doing fine. Do you want to talk to him? Hang on."

Putting her spoon down, she covered the mouthpiece and called to her five-year-old brother in the next room. She was answered by an immediate crash of what Leslie's trained ear knew to be Legos, and a pounding of pajama-clad feet.

"What?" panted a tiny blond-haired boy. His voice betrayed his annoyance with the interruption.

"Here, Travis. Talk to Daddy." Leslie handed the boy the phone. He awkwardly positioned it against his small head. Leslie bent down to hold it for him, and as he heard his father's voice, his blue eyes sparkled with delight and his attitude instantly changed.

"Daddy!" he cried. "Daddy, did you get me something?" Leslie couldn't help but smile. "Daddy, I built a big airplane, like the one you and Mommy flyed on! It's a 7-2-4-7-9-50. It's *real* big. But I broke part of it when I got up."

Travis intently studied the floor as he listened and began to nod slowly. "Yeah, I think I can have it fixed before you get home. I'll have to work hard. It'll probably take twenty-fifty hours. But I'll try. I love you, Daddy. Can I talk to Mama?"

Travis squinted his eyes as if trying to summon his mother to the phone. When he heard her voice, his face instantly relaxed. "Mama!" he squealed. "Mama, I've been good. Haven't I, Leslie?" Leslie smiled and nodded her approval. "See? Leslie said I been good. Did you get me something?"

He became quiet, and then broke out into a huge grin. "But, Mama, tell me *now*. I promise I'll pretend to be surprised. Please tell me! Okay. I love you, Mama. Here's Leslie."

Leslie took the phone, and Travis scampered back to his room. Leslie repositioned the receiver and stirred the noodles once more.

"He really has been an angel, Mom. I haven't had any problems. But tell me about your trip! How's the second honeymoon going? Is Dad still romantic enough after twenty-five years?"

Turning off the heat, Leslie picked up the pot and walked over to the sink. "That's just great! I hope you two enjoy your dinner. And don't forget to behave! I love you both. Travis and I are about to sit down to a late supper. . .Yeah, we got back late from the movie. We went to see that one with the animals . . .Uh-huh, the one he's been bugging us about since he saw the commercial. Well, he liked it, I guess. We may go out for ice cream later, if he wants to.

"Anyway, I guess I will let you two get on with your evening. Tell Daddy to make sure and open the doors for you. . . I love you, too, Mom. Give Dad my love. Talk to you later."

Leslie placed the phone back on the charger. After rinsing the spaghetti, she set the kitchen table for two. Placing the pasta and the sauce in the middle of the table, Leslie sneaked over to the open door of her little brother's room. Crouching near the ground, she stealthily poked her head around the corner and watched Travis rebuild his masterpiece. Suppressing a giggle, she began to crawl in on hands and knees. As Travis delicately placed the huge, multicolored configuration on the hardwood floor and began to search for an eluding component, Leslie reached out and tickled him.

Laughing and squealing, Travis tried in vain to fight off the attack. Leslie rolled over onto her back and propped him up in the air with her legs. "I'm gonna let go! Uh-oh, Travis, don't fall!" She held on to his stubby arms as he kicked his legs.

"Leslie, I saw you. You didn't sneak up on me. I saw you!"

"You did not! I'm a spy. You couldn't have seen me."

"I did! Really! Let me down, please!"

Leslie eyed the smiling child suspiciously. Narrowing her blue-green eyes, she demanded, "Why should I? You're not hungry, are you?"

"Yes! Yes, I am, Leslie." He tried his best to sound convincing.

"I don't think you are. No, Travis, I am, in fact, certain that you're not. You know why?"

"Why?"

"Because I specifically recall feeding you *yesterday*." Lowering her legs, Leslie brought the boy to the floor but quickly captured him in a tight hug.

"But, Leslie, you *have* to feed me! Mama said!" Travis continued to squirm, but she held him fast.

"She did?"

"Yes," he said matter-of-factly. "Mama *and* Daddy said you had to feed me. Every day."

"Every day? They did?" Leslie feigned confusion. "Hmmm . . .well, I guess I've got to, if Mom *and* Dad said to. It's a good thing I made a bunch of spaghetti then, isn't it?"

She picked him up and carried him on her hip as she turned off his bedroom light. Travis happily chanted a song about spaghetti, and Leslie placed him on the floor. "What do you want to drink, honey?"

"Orange juice," he proclaimed, climbing into his chair. Leslie brought down a plastic glass with a lid, filled it with orange juice, and placed it in front of him.

"I'm afraid we don't have any orange juice, sir. But, we do have some orange slime that I'm sure you'll find to your liking."

"Ewww. . .slime! Cool." Leslie laughed as he took a giant

gulp. "Hey, it *tastes* like orange juice." He looked down at the top of his lid, perplexed. "Leslie, is it really slime?"

"Yes, Travis, it is. I bought it especially for you this very morning." She blessed the food and then asked, "Do you like it?" She fixed his plate of pasta and sauce, carefully cutting the noodles and mixing it all together. Setting it before him, she awaited his answer with a look of intent interest.

Travis took another sip of his drink. "Yeah, I guess so. It's pretty good. Do you want some?" He extended his tiny hand. Leslie puckered her lips and shook her head violently.

"No, no, no. It says right on the bottle, 'Only for Five Year Olds Named Travis!' I can't drink it. I'm too old." Leslie spooned the meaty sauce onto her own plate of spaghetti.

"Your name isn't Travis, either," he pointed out thoughtfully.

Leslie's face assumed a puzzled look. "No, I suppose you're right. You know, you may get to be a spy yet. Hey," she whispered conspiratorially, "you wanna go out for ice cream?" Despite the fact that it was below freezing outside, ice cream was a treat always welcomed at the Heyward house. "It would be the perfect thing for spies. Who else would go eat ice cream in January?"

Travis leaned in close to her. "Okay. We'll be spies."

Leslie looked him over critically. "No, wait. You can't be a spy."

Travis looked wounded. "Why not, Leslie? I want to. Please?"

"No, no. It can't happen. You see, Travis, spies don't eat ice cream in pajamas. Spaghetti, maybe. Ice cream, never." Leslie put her fork on the table. "I guess we'll just have to stay home."

"I can change, Leslie! Then we can go! Please? Let me change," Travis pleaded.

"I suppose that would work. Yes, that should work nicely.

Okay. We can still go get ice cream. Just make sure you finish your spaghetti and your slime. Then we'll go pick out a spy outfit for you."

Travis looked pleased with himself. "Good. Thank you, Leslie. I'll be a good spy. I promise."

Leslie felt her heart swell with love for the little boy. "I know you will, honey. I trust you. Now hurry and finish up."

Leslie managed to twirl the last of her pasta onto her fork and eat it without getting it all over her white T-shirt. Travis's pajama top was another story.

Leslie scrutinized him for a moment. "Any of that food make it into your mouth, Travis?"

The little boy grinned a messy spaghetti smile and nodded. Strings of pasta fell from his pajama top as he replied, "Uh-huh, see?" He opened up his mouth, displaying for her the contents.

"Sorry I asked."

She cleared the table and sent Travis off to wash, which of course she had to complete when he returned still wearing a spaghetti sauce mustache. Within minutes, however, Travis was clad in black sweats. He insisted on wearing sunglasses. Leslie agreed that they did, indeed, complete his spy motif and loaded him into her teal Toyota. It was a good night, she thought. Turning on the car radio, Travis insisted on the *1812 Overture*, and they drove off to the ice cream shop, singing along with the orchestra.

☙

Leslie turned off the engine and looked over at the sleeping boy in the passenger's seat. Gently, she unbuckled his seat belt and then undid her own. Pulling him onto her lap, she cradled his limp body in her arms and managed to get out of the small car. Fumbling for her house key, she awkwardly unlocked the front door and switched on the lights.

Familiarity greeted her like an old friend. She had shared

this house with her parents for all of her twenty-four years, and in that time she had known nothing but happiness. Travis stirred in her arms, and she smiled, remembering the surprise he had caused with his birth. Her mother had given up on having any more children, although she and Aaron Heyward had wanted a half dozen or more. Travis had been born on her mother's fortieth birthday, and Peggy Heyward had proclaimed him the perfect gift.

Carrying her brother upstairs, Leslie readied him for bed, and after removing his sunglasses, she stood back for a moment and studied the angelic face. A small sigh escaped. He was so peaceful when he was asleep, yet twenty places at once when he was awake. She kissed him on the forehead and switched off the light.

"I wonder if I'll ever have a son," she murmured, glancing back at the door. The warm glow of the hall light fell across the boy's face like a muted spotlight. "If I do, I hope he's half as nice as you, Travis."

Downstairs, the silence of the evening seemed out of place for the house of Travis Heyward. She turned on the television and plopped down in an overstuffed chair.

Using the remote to run through several channels, she gave up. "Nothing's on," she said to no one in particular. Leaning over to the phone, she noticed she had a message. "Probably Aunt Margie," she said, playing the tape.

"Ms. Heyward, this is Detective Casey Holder with the Dallas Police Department. There's been an emergency here, and we need you to contact our office immediately. You can reach me at. . ."

Leslie's mind shut the tape out. Numb, she rewound it and played it again, just to make sure she had heard the man's voice correctly. In disbelief, she dialed the number left on the tape. It rang several times before a woman answered.

"Dallas Police Department. How may I direct your call?"

"I. . .I need to speak to Detective Holder," Leslie stammered.

"One moment. May I ask who's calling?" The woman's gravelly voice seemed unfeeling and empty. Just the way Leslie, herself, felt.

"This is Ms. Leslie Heyward. He called me while I was out and left a message that I should contact him immediately."

"Okay, I'll put you through." Leslie heard the phone ringing again and stared blindly at the television.

"Detective Holder here." A man's deep voice sharply filled her mind.

Leslie was forced back into reality. "Detective Holder, this is Leslie Heyward. You called about some emergency. Please tell me what this is about." She sounded more panicked than she wanted to, but she couldn't help herself.

"Ms. Heyward, how difficult would it be for you to come to Dallas right away?"

"What's going on? What's happened?"

"Well. . .that is to say. . ." The man paused, obviously uncomfortable with the task at hand. "Ms. Heyward, your parents were hit by a drunk driver this evening. It was head-on at about ninety miles per hour."

"Are they. . .are they okay?" she paused, trying to think. *Of course, they wouldn't be okay.* "Were they hurt badly?"

The man's voice seemed to lose its edge. "I'm sorry, Ms. Heyward. They were both killed."

Both? They're both dead?

"Ms. Heyward, are you there?"

She thought she'd spoken the words aloud. "Yes," she managed to whisper. "Are you sure that it was Peggy and Aaron Heyward who were killed?"

"Well, that's why I've called. I mean. . .I. . .well these things are never easy. We need you to come identify their belongings, and, well, we need you to bring their dental records."

"Dental records?"

"Yes, I'm afraid there was a fire and well. . .the bodies. . ." He left the rest unsaid.

"I understand," she said mechanically. "I'll leave in the morning if I can get hold of the dentist. I'll just need to get someone to watch my brother. . ." Her voice trailed off.

"Ma'am?"

"Yes, I'm sorry. Just tell me where to come. I'll be there sometime tomorrow afternoon."

"Certainly, Ms. Heyward."

*

"Hello?"

"Aunt Margie, it's Leslie. I need you to come over here right now."

"Les, what is it? Is it Travis? Is he okay?"

"Margie, Mom and Dad were in an accident tonight."

"What? How?" The obvious disbelief in her aunt's fearful tone left Leslie realizing she should have waited to explain until they were in person.

"I don't have many of the details," Leslie stalled.

"But surely they told you how it happened—where they've taken them."

"Look, this isn't the kind of thing we should discuss over the telephone. It's such a shock and I know—"

"Leslie, you aren't leveling with me," her aunt suddenly interrupted. "Just how bad was this accident, and don't you dare try to sugarcoat it for me."

Leslie felt tears come to her eyes as she broke the news. "They were killed, Aunt Margie. I have to go to Dallas tomorrow and identify their things. It was a drunk driver, head-on. The detective said it was a collision at about ninety miles per hour. I need you to watch Travis for me. Please."

"Oh, no!" Leslie heard Margie begin to sob. "Les, no! Not Peggy."

"Aunt Margie, please. Travis is asleep, and you can use the

guest room or sleep on the couch. I need you to do this. Please."

She knew the older woman was trying to compose herself. "Yes, Les, I'm on my way. You do whatever you need to do. I'll watch Travis for you. But what are we going to do about Crossroads?"

For the first time, Leslie thought about the coffee shop she co-owned with her parents. Now, it was hers. Hers. *Dear God,* she prayed, *help me make sense of it all.*

"Tomorrow is Sunday, Margie. The store will be closed anyway. I should be back Monday. Well, at least I hope I'll be back then. We'll just have to take turns running it while the other one watches Travis. I just can't do this right now. We'll figure it out later. Right now I'm too frazzled. I've got to make arrangements for the plane ticket, and then I have to call the dentist. Or should I call the dentist first? Oh, I don't know!"

"The dentist? Why the dentist?"

Leslie frowned and tried to think of a delicate way to explain. "They need the dental records for identification."

"Oh, my" was all Margie could say.

"Can you please come?" Leslie questioned one final time.

Margie sniffled. "I'm on my way. Don't go anywhere until I get there. We'll do this together. I can make calls while you're gone and tell everybody else."

"Thanks, Margie. I'll be here."

Leslie hung up the phone and began to cry softly into a pillow, trying to muffle her sobs. *I can't wake Travis,* she thought. Sheer dread flooded her mind. *How am I ever going to tell my poor baby brother?*

two

Kansas City International Airport was alive with action. The incessant hum of conversations reminded Darrin Malone of a cloud of angry bees. It was just as intimidating. Leaning closer into the partitioned phone booth, Darrin struggled to hear the busy signal on the other end of the line. He was used to it by now. After attempting to place a call for the last forty-five minutes, he had pretty much given up on Laurelin ever answering.

"Come on, Lin, hang up the phone," he pleaded to the pulsing tone. "I don't have time for this!" He placed the receiver back on the hook and sighed. Running his fingers through his dark brown hair, he contemplated just getting on the plane without calling her. Surely she'd understand. He shook his head. No, she wouldn't. Laurelin wouldn't understand because it didn't concern her. It wouldn't matter to her. "What a way to think about the woman who will be my wife!" he muttered. He dialed her number again, this time more out of guilt than consideration. Finally, the line was not occupied.

"Hello?" A perky voice filled his mind.

"Lin, it's Darrin."

"Darrin, where are you, sweetie? You *are* still going to dinner with me tonight, aren't you?"

"That's why I called. I, uh, have to fly to Dallas this morning. It's an emergency. I'm sorry, but I can't take you to dinner tonight." Darrin waited for the inevitable vituperation of his slighted fiancée.

"What? Oh, no, mister. You are *not* going anywhere tonight unless it's with me. Do you have any idea how many appointments I made for this? Nails, hair, everything! You simply

14

cannot do this to me."

"Honey, I know. I understand, and I will make it up to you, I promise. Please understand *me*. You know I wouldn't cancel if I didn't absolutely have to. Don't take this personally. It has nothing to do with you. I will explain everything later. It shouldn't take any longer than a day, maybe two. We'll go out when I get back."

"Oh, *fabulous,* Darrin. Positively fabulous. You are so inconsiderate sometimes. I honestly don't know if I will ever be able to marry you. You just don't think about *me*." Laurelin stopped to take a breath. "So just what do you propose I do all evening? Hmmm? Did *that* fit into your plans? Did it ever occur to you that I'll be sitting around all night, watching stupid sitcoms? No, of course it didn't. I can't believe you can treat me like this and just expect me to take it."

"Look, Laurelin, I have tried to be congenial about this and respect your feelings. However, instead of being a grown-up about this, you have wasted my time with the rantings of a spoiled high school girl who doesn't get to go to the prom. It really is ridiculous. It seems I spend more and more of my time trying to justify my actions to you. Now, my flight leaves in five minutes, and I hardly think the pilot will be sympathetic when I explain that he had to hold the flight so I could listen to my fiancée act like a child. I will call you when I get to Dallas, and we can discuss this then. For now, please trudge on like the trooper I know you are, and spare me the melodramatics."

Darrin stopped and took a deep breath. No doubt he'd crossed the line, but he didn't care. There was a time and a place for everything, and Laurelin would definitely have to learn that.

"I can't believe you! You are so. . .so. . ."

"So late. Now, if you'll excuse me, I have a flight to catch. Why don't you go sit down and figure out some nasty, yet oddly witty names to call me and write them down so you don't forget them when I call you later? Good-bye."

Darrin waited for her to say the same, but instead, he was left listening to a dead line. She'd hung up on him. Again. What difference did it make? Darrin replaced the receiver and gathered up his carry-on bag. Three minutes to go. Wonderful. Dashing through the labyrinth of security, Darrin finally boarded his plane.

There was one thought on his mind—marriage to Laurelin was steadily losing its appeal.

&

Darrin fastened his seat belt and melted into the chair. Closing his eyes, he tried desperately to clear his mind but couldn't. His life was in utter turmoil, and he had no control. It was not a position he relished.

When had Laurelin started to irritate him so? He tried to think back to better times between them, but frankly there weren't that many to reflect on. Laurelin had been thrown at him in a rather unavoidable manner, and like a hound to the fox, she had taken it from there. They'd met at the grand opening of his antique store, Elysium. The shop was designed to carry not only the finest American antiques, but also specialized European articles. This immediately appealed to Laurelin, whose freelance interior design work could greatly benefit by having such lovely articles at her fingertips.

From that first moment, however, Darrin knew Laurelin had been after more than a good discount on antiques. She'd managed to artfully maneuver herself so completely into Darrin's life that when he found himself needing to either shut down the shop while he went to Paris or send someone in his place to inspect a new cache of antiques, Laurelin offered to keep the home fires burning.

After that, there was no stopping her. She made herself indispensable in ways that Darrin found impossible, or at least difficult, to refuse. The business was consuming his days and nights, and taking on a partner or at least an associate seemed the smart and reasonable thing to do. Laurelin made certain that Darrin was completely charmed by her looks, her manners, and her personality, and it wasn't hard to believe her capable of being all the things he wanted her to be.

He sighed, wondering why the plane delayed its takeoff. It was bad enough to carry the added burden of Laurelin's anger, but facing what he had to deal with in Dallas was enough to make him jump out of his seat and flee the plane. *Why did everything have to fall apart at the same time?*

"This is your seat," the flight attendant announced, and Darrin glanced up in time to find the attendant and an attractive, petite blond hovering beside him.

He could see that the seat in question was the only empty place in first class, and he was blocking access to it. "I'm sorry," he said and unbuckled his seat belt. Getting to his feet, he let the young woman into the window seat and returned to his position. Rebuckling the belt, he turned to find the woman looking around her with a rather startled expression of helplessness.

"Do you fly often?" he asked casually, wondering if it might just be first-time-flyer jitters.

"Not really," she whispered. "Not for a while."

He noticed that she was clutching her carry-on bag as if it might suddenly escape her hold. "Would you like me to put that in the overhead compartment for you?" he questioned, nodding to the bag.

"No!" she exclaimed, then seemed to force herself to relax. "I mean. . .that is. . .I want to keep it close."

"You'll have to put it under the seat then," he told her in a conspiratorial manner and grinned. "It's rumored that the plane can't achieve lift without the baggage properly stowed."

She looked at him with wide, reddened eyes as if trying to decide whether he was telling the truth or not. Darrin felt almost guilty for having made the joke. He shrugged and smiled again. "Sorry. I was just trying to humor you."

She nodded and loosened her hold on the bag. "I guess you're right," she murmured and slipped the bag under the seat in front of her.

The flight attendants were instructed to prepare the cabin for takeoff, and after running through their routine of seat belt instructions and nearest exits, they made their way through the cabin for one final check. Darrin had fully planned to sit back and doze for the hour-and-ten-minute flight, but with the woman at his side now softly weeping into a well-spent tissue, he couldn't begin to relax. For some reason, his heart went out to the petite blond. She looked exactly the way he felt on the inside.

Once the plane had taken off, Darrin rummaged around his own carry-on bag and produced a monogrammed handkerchief. Sheepishly, he offered it to her, his look a cross between consuming sympathy and embarrassment. "Here. This won't fall apart on you like that paper."

Surprisingly, she reached for it and dabbed at her blue-green eyes. He found they were more brilliant against the redness caused by her tears and was momentarily speechless.

"Thank you," she squeaked.

"No problem," he said, immediately composing himself. "My name is Darrin Malone. If there's anything else I can do for you, don't hesitate to ask. I'm headed for Dallas." At this, the woman's tears began anew. After a brief, yet heart-wrenching deluge, she managed to pull herself together.

"I'm going to Dallas, too. My parents were killed in a car accident down there." She paused, as if listening to herself. Then, almost as an afterthought, she offered her right hand. "I'm Leslie Heyward."

Darrin was stunned into silence. "I'm so sorry" was all he could say. His mind blurred with unspoken questions. *And I offered to help this woman? What could I possibly do to aid her?* Feeling very awkward, Darrin stared at the headrest of the seat in front of him. *Should I ask her for more details? Or would that only make her feel worse?*

As if knowing the dilemma she'd created, the woman spoke again. "They were there for their twenty-fifth wedding anniversary."

Darrin turned his gaze to the woman, surveying her jeans and pale blue sweatshirt. She looked as though she hadn't slept for at least a day or so, and her face had a soft, yet haggard appearance. Makeupless and ponytailed, Leslie Heyward was still one of the most beautiful women Darrin had ever seen.

"I had just talked to them on the phone before they left for dinner last night. . ." Her voice trailed off.

"Last night? How awful."

He watched as she fought off another round of tears. "Yes," she nodded. "I was babysitting, and we went out for ice cream. When I got home, there was a message for me to contact the police, so I did and—" She stopped abruptly. "I'm sorry. I'm rambling. It's just such a shock." She appeared almost embarrassed by her grief. "Please forgive me."

"It's no problem, Ms. Heyward, really. I don't mind listening. I can tell that you must have loved them very much."

"Please, call me Leslie. I don't feel very much like a 'Ms. Heyward' right now. Though I'm sure I'll hear a lot of it in the days to come." For several moments, neither one said anything. Then Leslie added, "Anyway, at least I know they're in heaven, and that comforts me."

"They were Christians, then?" Darrin asked.

Leslie nodded emphatically. "Yes, Mom and Dad were strong Christians. I was brought up in a very loving and supportive environment. We went to church together, and Mom led a women's Bible study group, and. . ." Tears began to streak her face again.

"It's good that you have that kind of faith," Darrin encouraged. "It will, no doubt, ease a lot of the pain to come if you know where they are."

Leslie looked up suddenly at him. "Are you a Christian?" She seemed almost pleading.

"Yes, I am." He noticed a sense of relief washing over her and decided not to add that while he considered himself a Christian, he knew he was sorely lacking in that area.

"I'm glad."

Darrin waited for some further comment, but none came. It was as if with that matter settled, Leslie had climbed back into her own private world and locked the door behind her. Darrin leaned back against the thickly cushioned seat and closed his eyes. Laurelin found his faith a pain—something to be dealt with only when absolutely necessary. Yet this stranger, this pain-filled young woman, was glad to know that he was a Christian. The comparison between the two women hit him like a load of bricks. Guiltily he remembered his mother's and grandmother's admonitions to only marry a woman of like faith.

"You'll never know a minute's peace," his grandmother had told him when he'd been nothing more than a gangly adolescent, "if you marry a woman who rejects God."

His mother's words had been similar. "You know the truth about God, Darrin," she had told him not long before dying. "And because you know the truth, God will expect you to live by that truth. Find a mate who will live that truth with you."

Darrin felt bittersweet pain at the memory. He'd somehow allowed all of his mother's and grandmother's wise words to vanish when Laurelin had arrived on the scene. *Oh, but that woman could make a man forget a great many important things,* he thought, with the weight of reality bearing down on him.

three

"Thank you for arriving so quickly, Ms. Heyward." Leslie studied the tall man, reading the pin that identified him as Detective Holder. "Please, come right this way."

She followed his commanding form into a spacious room with bare walls, several chairs, and a large table covered with odds and ends. The fluorescent lights provided a dreamlike quality in their illumination, and Leslie moved as though she were underwater. *Maybe this is a dream,* she thought hopefully. *Please, God, let it be a dream.* The fuzzy serenity of the scene was soon shattered as she began to recognize various items on the table.

Her mother's purse—she'd shopped for hours at the outlet mall back home, trying to find one with just the right compartments in just the right places, and Leslie had spent the afternoon laughing with and at her because of her finicky nature.

A black pump that, no doubt, belonged to her mom.

Two suitcases.

Suddenly, everything became blurry, and Leslie realized she was crying softly as she touched the items that represented her parents. Turning away, she felt a strong hand on her shoulder.

"Are you going to be all right, Ms. Heyward?" It was Detective Holder. She knew his voice now.

"Yes," she managed. "I just need some water, I think." Her throat felt tight and dry. Detective Holder left the room and reentered with a small Styrofoam cup. Leslie took a long drink and tried to clear her thoughts.

"Are those the dental records we requested?" Detective Holder asked, motioning to the envelope Leslie clutched with her purse.

21

"Yes." She looked at the envelope as though remembering it for the first time. She put the cup down and handed it to him.

"Thank you," he said. "I'm sure this will take care of everything." He wrote something across the top and put it aside. "Now, what we need you to do is positively identify these items. The purse and shoe were apparently expelled from the car at the point of impact. We found the rental car registration inside the purse and traced the names to their hotel. The suitcases are from there. Do you think you can handle it?"

His voice was soothing, almost coddling, as though he were speaking to a child. Leslie didn't take offense. His manner was exactly what she needed at that moment, and she was grateful for his compassion.

"I think so." She walked over to the table again. "That's my mother's purse. I was with her when she bought it." She caressed the handbag, remembering the afternoon. "I think those are Mom's shoes, and that looks like their suitcases."

"You can go ahead and open it, if you think the contents will confirm it for you."

Gingerly, she snapped the clasps, and her eyes fell upon neatly folded piles of clothes. There was Mom's favorite red sweater and the tie that Travis picked out for Daddy's Christmas present. Leslie smiled as she fingered the obnoxious yellow and orange patterned material, remembering how proudly her father had worn it. Travis had insisted it was "just the thing for Dallas," and Aaron had obligingly packed it so as not to offend his son's undeveloped sense of style.

Digging deeper, she found a brown paper sack and opened it. Inside, she saw an electronic children's book about Texas. It was unmistakably intended for Travis. Slamming down the lid, she fought back tears and managed to choke out, "Yes, these things are all theirs."

She looked up, as if seeking reassurance that she had done

well. Detective Holder nodded and scribbled a few words onto a clipboard. Leslie exhaled sharply. Had she been holding her breath? When the detective motioned her out of the room, she followed without question, anxious to be out of the surrealism of her parents' possessions.

"Now, if you'll have a seat in here." He opened a door across the hallway. "I'll get these dental records on their way to the coroner, and then I'll be right back to speak with you."

Numb, Leslie sat down in an oversized blue chair. She vaguely remembered from college psychology that blue was supposed to calm the mind. She hoped it would work for her but felt no immediate relief. Studying the cornflower velveteen, she tried desperately to feel the effects of its color. Her search for solace was interrupted abruptly by the entrance of Detective Holder, and her head jerked up as though she'd been slapped.

"Okay, Ms. Heyward. What I'm going to do now is explain what happened, and then I need you to tell me how you want things arranged. Okay?" He seemed genuinely concerned, his gunmetal blue eyes trying to read what she was feeling. His mouth appeared to be in a perpetual frown, as though he'd been surrounded by death and despair for too long to remember how to smile.

"Yes, please tell me what happened." She sat back, deep into the chair, seeking comfort and security in the abundant stuffing, bracing herself.

"Well, they were driving toward their hotel at around nine o'clock, Saturday night. From the other direction, a drunk driver jumped the curb and hit the rental car at approximately ninety miles per hour. Your parents and the other driver were killed instantly. They didn't suffer. In fact, they probably never even knew what happened."

Leslie nodded, glad to know they hadn't been in prolonged pain.

The detective continued. "The rental car burst into flames. Sparks and gasoline were to blame most likely. The police arrived shortly after 9:07, but by that time, the bodies were unrecognizable. They were able to salvage a few of the items, and from them, we were able to locate their hotel. That's where most of the items are from—the ones you identified in the other room."

He seemed to wince a bit before he went on. "Now, Ms. Heyward, I don't know how you feel about dealing with the remains, but I will be honest with you. I wouldn't want you, or anyone else for that matter, to see them as they are. I suggest that you go ahead and allow them to be cremated, just for the sake of preserving their memories."

"I don't, that is to say, my family doesn't have a lot of money to spend." She hated the way the words sounded. Funerals were supposed to be a final good-bye to the physical evidence of your loved ones. Leslie felt frustrated by the fact that money would need to be an issue.

"I understand. I'm sure we can work out all the details, however," the detective told her. "The Dallas Police Department will be more than happy to help you arrange for something to be done here. Frankly, a simple cremation will be the cheapest way to go. You avoid the big cost of transporting coffins. . ." His voice trailed off as though he could see how his words were hitting her. "We'll try to do what we can to help. But it is your decision, and it will be respected."

Leslie couldn't find any words. She'd never considered planning her mother and father's funeral. She'd always assumed they would be old and that one or the other of them would be left alive to help her make the decisions. Cremation was something she'd never thought about, but given the details that Detective Holder had just shared, Leslie knew he was right. Travis couldn't see them like that. He wouldn't understand that the charred and mangled bodies weren't really his parents anymore. Aunt Margie didn't need to see them that way, either. And Leslie herself knew that she certainly didn't want to have her final memories of her parents to be in that form.

"I suppose you're right, Detective Holder. It would be best to have them cremated here, and I will just fly home with the urns and try to explain it to the family. Please, just get me the paperwork, and I'll sign it."

She felt exhausted and her jean-clad legs felt like they were made of lead. Detective Holder gave her his best encouraging smile-frown and left the room.

Leslie felt overwhelmed. For the first time, she had all the information—and all the pain. Before Detective Holder's explanation, it was almost as if it hadn't happen. Now, how could she deny the cold, hard facts? She had seen her parents' things—lifeless reminders of the people who'd once been so very much alive. She had heard the police account—official, unemotional words. She had consented to their cremation. It was real. And she was alone.

Detective Holder reappeared, and Leslie looked up at him. "So now what?" she asked, feeling at a loss.

"Have you checked into a hotel yet?"

"No," she said, shaking her head. "I came right here from the airport. I didn't even think about needing a place to stay."

"That's not a problem," the man replied. "I can have you put up nearby."

"Is that absolutely necessary? I mean. . .I. . .well. . ."

He appeared to redden a bit as if embarrassed for her. "I know money's a factor, but don't worry about it. It'll be taken care of."

Leslie could only nod. "How long will I have to be here?"

"Well, this is Sunday. We'll have the coroner confirm things in the morning and get the bodies right over to a funeral home. I'll see to it that the matter is taken care of in an expeditious fashion. There's no reason you should have to wait around here for more than a day, two at the most."

Nodding her understanding, Leslie next turned to the stack of forms Detective Holder had brought with him.

≥

That night, after a quick call to her aunt, Leslie lay awake for a long time. The hotel bed was comfortable enough, but her mind wouldn't let her relax. What were they going to do now? Suddenly she was responsible for everything. It only proved to her how sheltered a life she'd lived. Her parents had always been good to give her the freedom to explore and come of age, but they'd also given her a stable family to count on. To be secure in. Now that was gone, and Leslie felt rather like someone had just pulled the rug from beneath her feet.

Could she possibly pick herself back up much less pull together the rest of the broken pieces of their lives? Could she take over the role of guardian to Travis?

The thought of her little brother caused a sob to escape from her throat. *Poor little guy. He has no idea what has happened.*

"Oh, God," she moaned the prayer, "how can I ever help him past this? How do you tell a five year old that his parents are never coming back to him?" She cried softly into the pillow, wishing against all other desires that this nightmare could be a mistake. What bliss it would be to have the detective call her in the morning and say that the records hadn't matched and that her parents were safely alive and well.

She wiped her tears and wondered for a moment if this might be a possibility. Maybe there had been a mistake. Maybe. . .

≥

It was after ten the next morning when Leslie finally awoke with a splitting headache and swollen eyes. For a moment, it all seemed to have just been a bad dream, yet even as she focused on the room around her, Leslie knew better. She yawned and stretched, feeling little strength to climb out from under the covers. She hadn't eaten in over twenty-four hours and while her hunger was clearly absent, the weakness was not.

She considered calling room service when the telephone rang, startling her. Hesitantly she went to pick it up.

"Hello?"

"Leslie?" It was Aunt Margie.

"Hi, Margie."

"How's it going? Have you heard anything yet?"

"No, I'm afraid not. Detective Holder said he'd push things through as quickly as possible, and I have a standby seat on the 5:30 flight out of Dallas, just in case everything can be handled in time." Leslie paused and took a deep breath. "How's Travis?"

"He's fine. I haven't told him much of anything. I just mentioned that you had to take care of some business and that hopefully you would be home tonight."

"Oh, Margie, how in the world am I ever going to explain this to him? He's only five. What can life and death mean to a five year old? He probably will think that they're just dead today and that they'll be back tomorrow. I can just see having to deal with this over and over and over again, and I don't know if I have the strength to do that."

"You can find that strength in God," Margie replied. "I know after my Bill died, it was almost more than I could bear, but somehow my faith in God got me through the rough times. God will see us through this as well. He's always with us."

"Then where was He when Mom and Dad were killed?" Leslie asked bitterly.

"Standing with open arms to welcome them home," Margie answered, her voice cracking with emotion.

Leslie nodded to the empty room. She knew that Margie spoke the truth. She knew she could trust God, even though all seemed lost. "This isn't going to be easy," she murmured.

"No, but we have each other, and I hope you know that I'm here for you and Travis. Together we can help each other stay strong, and together we can help each other find healing."

"Thanks, Margie. I guess I needed to hear that."

"Would you like me to get in touch with the pastor? I can get things started for the funeral if that would be of help to you."

"It would be wonderful," Leslie said, a heavy sigh escaping her. "Plan out whatever you think would be best." She gritted her teeth together, remembering that she'd not explained to Margie about the cremation. "Margie, there's something you need to know."

"What is it?"

"Well, you knew that the bodies were burned." She stopped and tried to push aside the hideous images that came to mind. "Detective Holder said it would be best that we not see them like that, and I. . .well. . .I signed the papers to have them cremated. I didn't even see them myself."

Margie was silent for several moments before answering. "I think you did the right thing. I suppose it will be hard for Travis to understand. They say it's much easier to deal with death if you actually can say good-bye to your loved one face to face. You know, see the body, the casket, and so forth."

"Yes, I know," Leslie admitted, having recalled reading about that very thing. "But this couldn't be helped. I suppose we'll just have to make it work in some other fashion for Travis. I can't imagine that giving him all the gory details would be healthy."

"Maybe not, but don't lie to him. If he asks, tell him the truth. You don't have to get graphic in order to do that, but he'll forever feel betrayed if he finds out that you sugar-coated it or outright lied."

"I'll keep that in mind. Look, I'd better get off of here. You know, in case they try to call me."

"I understand," Margie answered. "Les?"

"Yes?"

"You aren't alone. Remember that. God is by your side every step of the way."

Leslie smiled and felt her nerves steady a bit. "Thanks, Margie. I'll remember."

four

Darrin Malone let the steaming water rush over his face. The powerful jets of the hotel shower mingled with the warmth, and he felt his muscles untie themselves from the knots of the day's dilemmas. All his worries swirled down the drain. For the first time in days, Darrin knew peace.

Sighing deeply, he reached out and rotated the handle to "off." He'd no sooner stepped onto the cold linoleum of the bathroom floor, than he heard a muffled pounding. Quickly, he wrapped a towel around his waist and strode out into the main room of his suite.

Knock-knock-knock!

So much for peace.

"Yes?" Darrin questioned through the door. The peephole revealed two men: one in a rather rumpled-looking suit, the other in the uniform of a Dallas police officer.

"Mr. Malone, I'm Detective Holder with the Dallas Police Department, and this is Officer Daniels. If you wouldn't mind, we'd like to speak to you for a moment about your father." Both men held their badges up to the hole and waited.

Darrin grimaced, even though he knew why they'd come. Unlocking the bolt, he opened the door and ushered the officers inside. They promptly took a seat at the table next to the windows and turned to face him.

"I'm afraid you caught me coming out of the shower. If you don't mind, I'll get dressed," he said, grabbing a pair of jeans and a flannel shirt from the opened suitcase lying on the queen bed.

"No problem." The men waited in silence.

Within minutes, Darrin reemerged, buttoning the last few buttons of his shirt. He tucked in the flannel and took a seat in the wing-backed chair across from the table set.

"Well, let's hear it." It was like a bad play that Darrin was forced to relive every few months. Always his father would drink himself into oblivion and then wrap his car around a telephone pole or drive off an embankment. Usually he escaped with little or no damage done to his own body, but always the cars were totaled. This time was different, however. This time would be the last time.

"Please tell me," Darrin added, looking up to meet the detective's guarded expression, "that no one else was involved."

"I wish I could, Mr. Malone. But it's not that simple." Detective Holder paused as though trying to choose the perfect words to describe the most imperfect of situations.

"Who else." It was more of a statement than a question, and Darrin was well aware of the angry, yet pained resignation in his voice.

"Why don't I just explain it from the beginning, Mr. Malone? That way, there won't be any holes in the account and you can fully comprehend the circumstances." Darrin nodded his approval and settled back into the burgundy material of the chair. At least this was the last time his father could cause any harm. Not that it soothed any of the wounds he had left behind, but it comforted Darrin in an odd way.

Detective Holder looked over to Officer Daniels before beginning. He opened the file he had brought along and perused its contents. He anxiously fidgeted with the file folder's edge before continuing.

"Well, Mr. Malone, it seems that Saturday night your father, Michael Malone, became intoxicated and began driving at excessive speeds. Around nine o'clock, he turned onto a four-lane divided street, and his speed reached approximately ninety miles per hour. He lost control of the vehicle and jumped the median. Another car traveling in the opposite direction was hit head-on and burst into flames instantaneously. Michael Malone died on impact, as did the passengers of the other car."

Darrin's stomach churned, and his chest tightened. He gripped the sides of the chair in order to keep from leaping to his feet. Brutal images filled his mind, and he could almost smell the smoke of burning rubber and paint.

"Who were they?" he barely whispered.

"A vacationing couple from Lawrence, Kansas."

"Young? Old?" Darrin questioned, barely keeping his voice steady. In his mind the ugly truth painted itself in even more vivid scenes. Years of living with his father's alcoholism were coming back to haunt him. Haunt him in a way that smothered his very breath.

"They were middle-aged," the detective replied hesitantly.

Darrin nodded, trying to fit imagined faces to the victims. "Are they being cared for?"

Officer Daniels nodded. "Yes, but we need to know what you want done with your father's body, Mr. Malone." He shifted in his seat before continuing. "It is not a good idea, in my opinion, nor in the opinion of the Dallas Police Department, that you see him. The dental records checked out, but the rest of the late Mr. Malone is unrecognizable. The fire spread quickly, and while the department put out the flames as fast as they could, your father's car was. . ." His voice trailed off as he realized Darrin was no longer listening.

Tears of anger stung Darrin's eyes, and he fought to keep them back. *What do I want to do with the body?* he thought. *Make him an example! Show all of those high school kids how cool it is to drink and drive. Show them what is left behind when the party's over and somebody else is left to pick up the pieces. Hah! It'd be the first time my father ever taught anybody anything worthwhile.*

"Mr. Malone?"

Darrin snapped back into reality. "What do you suggest?" he managed. His anger was the only thing protecting him from grief.

"Well, like we suggested to the family of the Kansas couple, cremation is, in our eyes, the best alternative. We would be more than happy to arrange for it to be done here and ship the urn home with you as soon as possible. Of course, your decision will be abided by. We just need an answer."

Cremation? Yes, that would make sense. After all, there was a fire. Darrin nodded in agreement. "Cremation sounds acceptable. How soon can this be over and done with?"

"We can call over first thing tomorrow morning. You shouldn't have to be here more than a couple of days." He handed the folder to Officer Daniels, who scribbled a few words across the top of the sheet.

"We thank you for your time." Officer Daniels extended his hand as the two men rose in unison. Detective Holder did likewise, and Darrin followed them to the door. "We'll be in touch."

Closing the door behind them, Darrin felt his anger renew itself. "How could you, Dad? What were you thinking? Or did you even remember how to do that? You didn't just hurt yourself this time. You killed two innocent people, probably here on vacation to relax! Well, they're relaxing now, aren't they, Dad? Just like Mom. Only you didn't kill her as directly, now did you? You happened to use a little more discretion when you got her, didn't you? Just let news of your drunken escapades trickle back to her until it was finally too much, and her body just gave up.

"It wasn't enough to just let the cancer eat her away! You weren't happy unless you could be an intricate part of her suffering even after the separation. At least now you can't hurt anyone. At least now the world can rest easy knowing the

Great Mike Malone has finally done himself in like so many before him!"

Tears streamed down his face as he yelled into the empty room, screaming at the ghost of a man who was easier to talk to in death than he ever was in life.

Darrin fell to his knees in complete emotional exhaustion. "Dear God—what do I do now? How do I rid myself of this bitterness—this rage?" He thought immediately of the verses in Ephesians 4. Verses that had made him almost get up from the church services and run without ever looking back:

Let all bitterness, and wrath, and anger, and clamor, and evil speaking, be put away from you, with all malice: And be ye kind one to another, tenderhearted, forgiving one another, even as God for Christ's sake hath forgiven you.

"But God, how do you forgive this?" he cried. "How do you forgive the taking of another life? Innocent life that was murdered by the choice of a ruthless man. My father wasn't saved. He found his savior and religion in a fifth of whiskey." Hot tears of anger flooded his face.

How many times had he tried to make his father see the truth? How many times had he prayed for his father to find salvation? Yet it was as if each and every prayer went unheard. "Why, God? Why this? Why now? There is no good thing that can possibly come out of this."

He stilled his rage for a moment and remembered the Scriptures again. *Forgiving. . .as God for Christ's sake hath forgiven you.*

"But how, God?" Darrin asked, looking at the stark white ceiling. "How can I forgive him this? How can You? He didn't want forgiveness, so what possible good can it do me to forgive him now?"

"Forgive him for *Christ's* sake," a voice seemed to whisper within his heart.

"I don't know if I can," he murmured, and those words hurt perhaps more than anything his father had done. The Bible clearly told him what he must do, but his human nature argued against it. The last thing he wanted was another battle over his father.

"I'll try." He closed his eyes and drew a deep breath. "That's all I can do. For Your sake, Jesus, I will try to forgive him."

Minutes passed, and finally he composed himself. Reaching for the remote control, he turned on the television and sat dejectedly on the end of the bed. It was as hard as a concrete bench, he thought, but somehow it didn't seem to matter.

The television hummed to life, and as the color image formed, a perky brunette appeared on the screen. "And in North Dallas, last night a drunk driver crashed into an on-coming vehicle and both cars burst into flames. The driver and the occupants of the other automobile, a couple from Kansas, were killed instantly in a mass conflagration of fire, twisted steel, and carnage."

She reads it as though it's about a sale at Neiman Marcus, Darrin thought. *Is there no compassion anywhere?* Suddenly, his eyes were filled with photos of the deceased Kansas couple and of his father.

For a moment, Darrin was speechless. Studying the picture, he felt he vaguely recalled the woman. The eyes seemed the same, but the face was different. Altered somehow. This woman was older, but. . .

And then he knew.

"No!" he cried out. They were *her* parents. They were the Heywards. The family Leslie had lost. And his father was to blame. He threw the remote across the room and listened to it clatter against the dresser.

It wasn't as if the thought hadn't crossed his mind on the flight to Dallas. He'd easily put it aside, however. His father's accidents were usually in the wee hours of the morning, and usually no one else was involved. Well, that certainly wasn't the case this time, and now he couldn't deny the truth of his earlier suspicions.

He conjured to mind the young woman who'd cried so pathetically into his handkerchief. Blue eyes, or were they green, seemed to stare back in his memory. What would she say to him now?

He couldn't shake the picture of her sitting there beside him—so tiny and frightened. So young. Then he had a horrible feeling. How young was she? The couple shown on the television looked to be in their fifties. Surely she was old enough to deal with matters, or she'd not have been on that plane.

The television was rambling on about an all-out winter car sale when Darrin got up and switched it off. He found the remote behind the dresser and placed it on the bedside nightstand. Restlessness overtook him. He had to do something. He had to find out where Leslie was and somehow do something to make it right.

No, he couldn't make it right, but he might be able to make it better. Perhaps he could help her with the arrangements or offer to pay her expenses. He went into the bathroom to comb his still-damp hair. Then an even more troubling thought came to mind.

"She won't ever want to see you once she knows the truth," he told his reflection in the mirror. "Your father killed her parents. She'll never want anything to do with you."

He hung his head and gripped the counter. "Who could blame her?"

His anger was surging anew. His own likeness to his father didn't help much, and soon the image in the mirror blurred into a reminder of his dad. It was like some kind of psychological warfare was being fought within him. *I am my father's son*, he thought, and this truth caused him even more pain.

He pushed down thoughts of the past and buried his pain deep within. "I may be his son," he reasoned, "but I'm not like him. I'm not a killer!"

five

Leslie sat rigidly on the pinewood chair of one of the many dinette sets positioned around the coffee shop. *Her* coffee shop, she remembered painfully. Hers alone. Yet another responsibility. Yet another worry. But there would be plenty of time to think about all of that later.

Right now, she had to figure out a way to deal with Travis. She still hadn't told him the reason for her rush-rush trip to Texas. Nor had she offered any real explanation when she told him that he'd be spending the day with the next-door neighbors, the Richmonds. He was happy enough to comply, as their twins, Kyle and Laney, were his best friends, and the reality of a day at play with them left Travis without any need of the details.

Wearily, she brought her gaze to meet that of the haggard-looking woman who only slightly resembled her aunt. They exchanged glances for several minutes. Both gripped steaming mugs of flavored coffees, as though deriving strength from the heat. Leslie brought her cup to her lips and gingerly sipped. Anything to buy time.

She scanned the interior of Crossroads. In two hours, it would be open for business. In two short hours, she would have to face the real world again. Sighing deeply, she tried desperately to compose her thoughts.

"God was with them," Margie murmured, as if sensing Leslie's renewed apprehension.

Leslie's head snapped up.

"No, really, Les. He was good to take them home so quickly."

Leslie's emotions surged like water escaping a dam. "I'm so confused! I know that all things are supposed to work for the good of those who love God, but where is the good in this? Where is the justice or the reason? How do you explain to a five-year-old boy that God saw fit to take his mommy and daddy away, but that it's really okay because everything will work out if we trust in Him? You can't, Margie. You can't! I can't even find the strength to believe it.

"There are mountains of problems we haven't even seen, let alone tackled. There are social norms that must be abided by, all the while maintaining faith in a God who robs babies of their parents for no reason at all! And I'm left to pick up the pieces, just as alone and scared as Travis. But I don't get the sugarcoated version. I am left with facts and figures and explanations and bills and fear and anger and—"

Her voice abruptly stopped, and she looked down into the creamy tan of her coffee. When she looked up, she felt a cross between shame and utter defeat. Aunt Margie's tender eyes, glistening with tears, never left Leslie's face.

"Les, you're not alone. You have me, and like it or not, you have God. A God who cares very deeply for you and for what has happened to your parents. A God whose plans, while no doubt mysterious and vexating to us, are surely unfolding as they should. He knows you're hurting, but He can't help you until you allow Him to." Aunt Margie's soft, yet stern voice filled Leslie's head, but it couldn't manage to push out the questions or the pain.

"If He cares so much, how could He let this happen?" She knew she sounded more like a little girl demanding answers about a runaway cat than a twenty-four-year-old woman, but she couldn't help herself. The hurting was too intense, and her need for understanding burned inside her mind. She needed reassurance, yet wasn't willing to accept the promises being offered.

Margie shifted forward to scrutinize her niece. "Leslie Heyward, do you really believe that God killed your parents? You know better than that! My sister raised you to know the truth. Now this is painful and this is hard for us to comprehend. Well, guess what? We don't have to! The world will not end just because you do not fully understand why God has allowed certain things to happen. I know you're hurting, Leslie. I'm hurting, too! But you cannot allow that pain to blind you from what is real. If you give up on God now, what good are you going to be to Travis? What is he going to think when his big sister doesn't even buy the rhetoric she's offering as an explanation? He's not stupid. He may be young, but often the young are the first to figure things out, especially when it comes to honesty. I don't believe for one second that you could look that boy in the face and lie. And that's just what you'll be doing if you tell him this and don't believe it."

Her face seemed to soften a bit as she relaxed against the back of the chair. "Oh, Leslie. Look inside your heart and inside your soul. There lives a God who is merciful and loving, a God who longs for you to return to His arms, and a God who desires to comfort you, not alienate you. Don't abandon your faith just because He didn't run things by you first. It doesn't work that way. Now is when you need Him the most. If you push Him away, what are you left with? Bitterness? Resentment? What kind of guide will those feelings be? Where will they lead you? How will they comfort you in the deepest darkness of the night, when your soul is bared and your defenses are shattered? Think about that before you blame God for what has happened."

Leslie sat in stunned silence. She knew the truth. It didn't erase the pain, but had she really expected it to? Well, actually, yes. She had. Even though she was a grown woman, she still believed in the Santa Claus God. If you were good, He would bless your life with wondrous things. If you believed, you would be spared pain and suffering. Bad things happened only to bad people. Injustice was punishment, not an everyday occurrence. Not to real Christians.

But what had just happened?

Bad things had happened to good people. No one could believe fervently enough or pray hard enough to avoid tragedy. Not her, not her parents, not anyone. What was she left with? A God who allowed His people to suffer at the hands of a cruel world, with nothing more than this concept of "faith" to comfort them.

But she was also left with a God who had blessed her in many ways. He had given her loving parents and a secure home. He had surprised her and her parents with the gift of a blond, blue-eyed tornado of a boy. He had allowed her to be brought to the truth at a young age and had kept her from harm's way for the better part of her twenty-four years. And now, now that she was being tested and tried, she was going to give up? Just because the presents stopped coming and the party was over?

This is real life, she scolded herself. *There is pain and suffering at every turn, and I can't explain it or stop it. But I am forced to deal with it and to help those around me by being strong. Am I so confident that I don't need God? Hah! I'm anything but confident. But still, it is so much more difficult when the pain is your own.*

"Leslie?"

Margie's words brought her back to the coffee shop and away from her troubled thoughts. She slowly shook her head and fingered the handle of her mug.

"Margie, I'm sorry. I know that what you say is the truth. I know this even in the deepest, most secret parts of my heart. I know that I'm being weak and letting my anger rule me, but this hurts so much! I don't know how I'm going to explain this to Travis because I'm not sure how to explain it to myself."

"Then don't. Accept that it has happened, acknowledge that it cannot be changed, and go on living with the faith you had before, when everything was beautiful and all was right with the world. Leslie, either God is God, or you are. And I think we both know, beyond a shadow of a doubt, the answer to that one."

The older woman smiled. "I will be here for you when you need me. I will listen to you and I will comfort you, but I will not let you lie to yourself and blame God for what has happened. I will not let you use that as an excuse to give up and go your own way. I love you, and God loves you. And don't forget that there's a five-year-old whirlwind at home who thinks the world of you, too. Search your heart, read the Bible, and pray. There's nothing more you can do. In time, you will find peace in those things. No peace comes from harboring bitterness and pain."

Silence filled the shop. Leslie's thoughts churned endlessly. They always returned to one central theme. Travis. What was she going to tell her baby brother? How was she to explain this random tragedy? How could she possibly word it so that a five year old would understand?

"Margie? How am I going to let Travis know?"

The older woman shook her head slowly. "I don't know, Leslie. All I can tell you is, don't lie, but don't offer any more than is necessary. He doesn't need to be let in on all the gory details, but this shouldn't be written off, either. This is a very important issue. It may well come back to haunt you someday, no matter how you tell him. Above all, be honest with him."

"But do I say, 'Okay, Travis, we need to talk about Mommy and Daddy. They are not coming home because they now live in heaven'? Or do I say, 'Travis, something really bad has happened to Mommy and Daddy, and I need you to be a very strong boy about this'? Should I start positive and work my way to negative, or start negative and end with something optimistic? Margie, there are thousands of books written on this subject. How can I be expected to figure something out that psychologists are still arguing over?"

"Pray for guidance, Les. Let God give you the words to say. I am not fool enough to believe that there is any one right way to break this to him. Just do your best. That's all anyone can ask of you."

"No, Margie. They can, and often do, ask for a lot more than 'your best.' Your best is never, ever good enough, especially in instances like this. There will be friends, family, church members, and whoever else you can think of who will have a recipe for success when it comes to helping Travis cope. All of them will have ideas that merit consideration, but they can't all be abided by! My best in this situation is going to be someone else's 'Avoid at All Costs' scenario. This isn't me running a race or writing a paper. This is a child's well-being—his life— at stake.

"If I don't do the right thing, my best isn't going to matter much at all. That's why this is so scary. Helping a child deal with the death of his parents is not something you can learn from a book or a television special. It may help, but in the end, you're on your own. I just don't feel strong enough to deal with this."

"I know."

Margie offered no other word, and soon the silence threatened to destroy Leslie's sanity. How could she just open the coffee shop with business as usual? How could she smile and serve and pretend that a cup of espresso could solve any problem her clientele might have on their minds? She slammed the mug down harder than she'd intended.

"It just isn't fair," she said getting to her feet. "And please don't counter with 'Life's not fair.' I think I've learned that lesson well enough." She paused, knowing that she had inflicted wounds with her words. "Look, I know we need to be strong together in this, but I feel so angry. Down deep inside," she said, pounding a slim fist against her breast. "Right here, I feel as though a hard, black lump of hatred and anger is threatening to explode. That man, that drunken fool, killed my parents—your sister."

Leslie whirled around and stared at the homey, hand-painted menu that was affixed to the wall behind the counter. "He stole them from us. He chose to drink too much. Then he chose to drive his car in a drunken stupor. He had the final say, and he took my parents away from me."

"Moving the blame from God to that man isn't going to bring them back," Margie whispered softly.

Leslie turned and stared in disbelief. "What do you want from me? First I'm angry at God and you tell me not to be—that He's still my best bud and He'll never leave me. So I try to rationalize that a loving God allows hideous actions to take place while He's ultimately in charge of everything, and you admonish me not to refix the blame? I'm sorry, but that man did make a conscious decision, and that decision ended the life of my parents. No, blaming him won't bring them back, but it does help to keep my mind on something other than my questions for God."

Margie got up and came to Leslie. Gently, she put an arm around her niece's shoulders. Leslie could feel a bit of the anger fade, remembering times when her mother had done the exact same thing. "Leslie, we have to go forward. Sitting here, wallowing in our self-pity is going to accomplish very little. You are angry. I am angry. It's something we must deal with, and I'm certain that each of us will have to deal with it in our own way."

Leslie felt tears come to her eyes. Why was it just when she figured herself to be all cried out, something would come along to prove her wrong?

Margie squeezed her shoulders. "Les, God knows you're

mad. You don't have to feel guilty or try to hide it from Him. Take it to Him and talk it through."

Leslie looked quite seriously at Margie. "They'll still be dead," she whispered.

"Yes. Yes, they will." Margie's reply came accompanied with her own tears. "But they wouldn't want this for you, and you know that full well. If that's the only thread that you have to grasp onto, then take it. Do this in honor of them, even if you can't find the strength to do it for yourself. Do it for Travis. He's going to need you now more than ever. You're literally his only link to them. Oh, I know, I'm his aunt and his mother's sister, but it isn't the same. You're the one he will depend upon. Remember that."

"But don't you see," Leslie said, pulling away, "that's all I can remember. He's going to look up at me with those huge eyes and say, 'But how can I believe what you say is true anymore? You said they'd come home and they never will again.' Believe me, Margie, I've played this thing over and over in my head. He's not ready for something like this."

"Neither were you, nor, for that matter, me. But he'll deal with it, just as we have. Hiding here at the shop isn't going to make matters any easier."

"We have to keep Crossroads open," Leslie answered curtly. "We aren't made of money, and the funeral is going to cost quite a pretty penny in spite of the fact that they. . ." Her words faded. She didn't even want to say the word *cremation*.

"Les," Margie came to stand directly in front of her, "we will get through this, and we will either fall completely apart or we will be stronger. Part of it is up to us. Our choice." She paused and once again placed her hands on Leslie. This time she tenderly touched Leslie's face and held her fast. "I'll stay here and open the shop, but you need to go to Travis. What if one of the Richmond kids overhears their parents talking and says something to Travis before you get a chance to speak to him? He's going to need to hear this from you, not from neighbors or friends."

Leslie swallowed down the painful lump in her throat. "You're right."

Margie nodded. "I know you would avoid this forever if you could."

"I wish—"

Margie put her finger to Leslie's lips. "I know. But what has happened has happened. And what you have to do now won't go away. Travis needs you. Will you leave him behind? Leave him in the same way that he will probably believe his parents left him?"

"No—never." Resignation washed over Leslie. What was it Thoreau had said about resignation? Oh, yes, 'What is called resignation is confirmed desperation.' That was exactly how she felt. Desperate. Desperate to see this thing over and done with. Desperate to know that Travis would survive the loss of his parents. Desperate to know that she would survive their loss as well.

❧

Leslie sat comfortably in the chair that had always been called Daddy's chair and cradled Travis in her arms. He didn't understand, nor had she expected him to.

"But why did they go away?" he asked, his voice strangely void of its usual rambunctious delight.

"Because it was time for them to go," Leslie offered, knowing it was a question she hadn't answered for herself. "We can't know all the answers, Travis. It's kind of like we're reading a big, big book called *Life*. We can only know what's happening on one page at a time, and we can't skip to the end to check on how things turn out."

"Is it like when Samson died?"

Samson had been their tabby cat. A year ago, Samson had lounged lazily under the family car in order to avoid the stifling heat of a Kansas summer sun. Their mother hadn't realized he was positioned just behind the front wheel of the car when she backed out. She ran over him, killing him instantly, and then spent the next few weeks ridden with guilt.

"In a way," Leslie began, "it's like when Samson died. That was an accident, and no one wanted him to die. Mommy and Daddy died in an accident, too, and no one wanted them to die."

"Does it hurt to die?" Travis asked, his voice now starting to quiver with emotion.

"It didn't hurt Mommy and Daddy when they died. It happened so fast that the police said they didn't even know anything bad was going to happen."

"And they're never coming back?"

"Well, not to earth, anyway. But we'll see them in heaven when we go to live with Jesus," Leslie answered softly. She prayed that he could somehow take in the information and make sense of it.

"Can we go to heaven now?"

Leslie felt her eyes fill with tears. Oh, if only they could just go to heaven now. If only she could press a button and announce that God could send a celestial chariot anytime. Or better yet, request to be beamed up as those science fiction shows did all the time.

"No, Travis. We have to wait until it's time for us to go to heaven. We don't know when God will be ready for us to come to heaven, but when He is, when we die, it will be all right because going to heaven is the very best gift of all."

Travis suddenly pushed away from her and jumped out of the chair. "But I want to go now! I want to go with Mommy and Daddy." He looked enraged, and Leslie was shocked by the transformation.

"But, sweetie, we can't. God isn't ready for us to come to heaven just yet."

"Then I want Mommy and Daddy to come back here. If I can't go, then I don't want them to go."

Leslie leaned forward and tried to reach a hand to her brother, but he pulled away. "I know how you feel, Travis. I feel the same way. But now, it's you and me and Aunt Margie, and together we have to stay here and keep trusting Jesus to help us. We'll miss them a lot, but we have each other. And when we miss them together, it won't seem near as bad as missing them alone."

Travis's lower lip jutted out. He was very close to crying, yet Leslie noted the restraint he practiced. "Please come here, Travis. Let me hold you."

"No! I'm not a baby." He ran off to his room, refusing any further discussion.

Leslie got up to go after him, but just then the telephone rang. Wearily, she picked it up. "Hello? Yes, this is she."

It was the funeral home. Leslie listened intently as an ancient sounding man went over the details of the funeral arrangements. He rattled on about the chapel usage and the cost of the organist, and after that some mention was made about family cars and how many would be attending so that announcements could be printed up.

"Wait a minute," Leslie interrupted. "What kind of cost are we talking here?" She suddenly realized for the first time that Margie had said nothing of the plans she'd put in motion. Cost had never been discussed, and Leslie knew it was going to be a major factor in planning the funeral of her parents.

The man seemed hesitant to discuss money over the telephone, but Leslie finally wore him down and got an item by item total.

"Well," Leslie said, looking at the figures she'd just written, "this is costing a great deal more than we'd planned on. For the time, I'd appreciate it if you would do nothing more." She paused. "Yes, I know these things take time and planning, but apparently they take a great deal of money as well."

She listened as the man explained why money should be the very least of her concerns at a time like this. Leslie felt herself burning with anger as he hinted a lack of caring on her part was causing her to suggest that cost dictate the funeral arrangements.

Finally, she could take no more. "I'm sorry that we bothered you. We won't be needing your services after all." She hung up the phone.

"Now what do I do?" she wondered aloud. "Aunt Margie will probably be furious with me. After all, she's the one who called them." A million thoughts raced through her mind. Her mother had always said that if anything happened to them, the shoebox in the basement would have all of their papers, including the deed to the house and the shop, as well as their wills. With a sigh, Leslie knew what she had to do, but facing up to it was almost more than she could bear. Then, too, there was Travis.

She strained an ear for any sound of the boy, but he'd closed his bedroom door and Leslie could hear nothing. *Give him some time,* a voice seemed to whisper to her heart.

Leslie started up, then thought better of it and sat down on the carpeted stairs to think. It was probably a good thing there was so much for adults to do at a time like this. It kept their minds busy, as well as their hands. But what of five year olds? What did they do at times like this? Should she give Travis a series of tasks to fulfill? Make him a part of the arrangements? Or would that only make it harder for him? Should she go try to talk to him again? Or did he need to search the silence to find his own answers?

"Oh, God," she cried, burying her face in her hands, "what do I do?"

six

Darrin was thankful for his many years of flying experience. When it came to boarding a plane, he was a pro. He could aimlessly wander through the routine without giving much thought to the actions he performed. There was comfort in such experience. Experience lent itself to routine, and routine allowed his mind to wander to other things, like Leslie.

After the plane touched down in Kansas City, Darrin collected his things and absentmindedly boarded one of the many airport shuttles. Grief and guilt washed over him in waves as he considered the situation in full. His mind could still hardly conceive that the nightmare of the past two days had actually happened. First, the sadness—the overwhelming loss that drenched his mind and soul. Sadness for the teary-faced woman who would have to wait for eternity in order to see her parents again. This sadness was quickly followed by shame and guilt, and then the melancholy would return. The turbulence of his emotions made him feel sick.

The shuttle pulled alongside his parking lot, and Darrin was soon behind the wheel of his car, merging with other travelers onto the interstate. He drove dejectedly through the heavy traffic and made his way toward his apartment outside Kansas City. The silence seemed too much to handle, so he switched on the radio to fill the consuming void. Mindless tunes poured out of the speakers, and for a moment, Darrin forced himself to think of nothing at all. But reality would not be ignored for long. Soon the pain and the remorse assaulted him once more and demanded to be dealt with.

"Oh, Lord," he prayed aloud, "what am I supposed to do? I

know there must be something I can do to help this woman. I have to try! It's my fault—it was my father."

Money. He could offer money. That's all he was really good for. And he had plenty of it. Yes, he would find her and offer financial assistance. Surely she could use it. Paying for a double funeral wouldn't be easy. But how would he explain it? How could he justify his interest in her well-being without revealing his relationship to her grief?

Darrin expertly navigated the winding streets of the busy Kansas City neighborhood and made his way to his apartment complex. Barely fitting his sports car between two inconsiderately parked vehicles, he squeezed out of the ten-inch opening he had managed to create without touching the immaculate Cadillac on his left.

"Please don't let it have an alarm," he repeated softly, over and over. He didn't feel like dealing with the attention of a sensory-activated alarm system that would, no doubt, yield bells or sirens or robotic voices. He just wanted to be anonymous and hide inside his own world for a little longer.

All hopes of quiet contemplation were dashed as soon as his eyes fell on the red convertible Mustang. Laurelin. She was waiting in his apartment. Why had he ever given her the key? Heaving a sigh, Darrin debated whether or not he should just turn around and leave. He didn't feel like dealing with her or her plans. Not now. Not ever, really.

For the past two days, their relationship had begun to weigh heavy on his heart. Not that it hadn't bothered him for quite a while. He had just been able to mask it better. Now, with the Heywards consuming his energies, he had very little tolerance for the materialistic rantings of the lovely Ms. Firth.

She didn't even know about his father, which in and of itself would prove interesting. Before, he'd implied that his father was no longer in his world, which was true. But Darrin knew that Laurelin had believed his father to be long dead and gone to whatever place Laurelin believed people went. With the ghost of such an undesirable character threatening her pristine family tree, she might very well break off the engagement herself.

"Oh, if it were only that easy," he muttered, making his way up the flights of stairs.

⁂

"Just where have you been?"

Darrin had barely unlocked the door before the vituperations of a slighted Laurelin began. He didn't bother to answer. It wouldn't matter, he knew, because until she had gotten her initial assault of words in, he would never be able to offer up even the most meager of explanations.

"Just what do you mean, leaving me alone for two days? The Andrews party was last night. I had to go alone. Alone. Me! I had to show up all alone and go home all alone and listen to everybody ask me where in the world you were and why you weren't at the party. And that was worse yet, because I didn't *know* why you weren't at the party. I couldn't very well say, 'Oh, you know, he forgot to tell me what he was doing!' You simply have no idea how difficult it was. I had to make up something that would excuse your absence from their party. Are you listening to me?"

Darrin's head was partially inside his closet as he hung up his suit jacket. "Yes, dear," he answered in monotone.

"I thought it was just going to be a quick overnight. But no, you were gone for two days. Just what was I supposed to do with myself for those two days?" Well-manicured hands rested upon slender hips, and Laurelin's brown eyes were dark and furious.

"Well, I hope you went to work at the shop," Darrin said casually, as he picked up his bag and carried it into his bedroom.

"The *shop*? Is that all you think about, Darrin Malone? How can I be expected to babysit your antiques *and* plan a fabulous wedding?" She shook her head, the short light brown hair falling perfectly into place with each pouty turn. "Darrin, I'm not a magician. I need *time*. I need you here taking care of things so I have time to think. I was too worried about you to go to the shop. Besides, I had to call the caterer, and the florist, and my mother, and. . ."

Darrin held up his hand. "Just stop. I don't want to hear about it right now. I need to talk, and you need to listen. Understand?"

Laurelin's frown deepened. "How dare you talk to me like that! I am your fiancée, not a child!"

"Then quit acting like one and sit down." She turned from him and glided to the nearest overstuffed chair.

Darrin studied her for a moment. She looked very professional, and there was no denying her beauty. She was elegant and refined, her light brown hair styled just enough to allow movement while retaining its form. Her makeup was expertly applied and accentuated her sapphire jacket and skirt. Her long legs were trim and defined and seemed to have pantyhose surgically grafted to them. He couldn't remember the last time he'd seen her in a sundress or relaxing in a pair of cutoff shorts and a T-shirt. Granted, he was first drawn to her for her impeccable taste in clothes and antiques, but now, he couldn't help but think it would be nicer to be engaged to a person instead of a fashion doll.

"Well?" Laurelin's impatient voice brought him back to reality. "What is it that's *so* important that you have to take that tone with me?"

"Look," he began. "The reason I had to fly to Dallas at the last minute was because my father had died in a car accident."

"Your *father*? I thought your father was already dead. Well, at least I thought he was out of the picture. Why in the world should it matter to you *what* happens to him? You couldn't possibly have had much of a relationship if I thought he was dead all this time."

"Ah, Lin. Your compassion is overwhelming. It's a wonder I could manage being away from your sweetness for forty-eight hours." Darrin sighed in complete exasperation. They were headed for another major fight at this rate, and that was the last thing he needed. Leaving his bags, he motioned her back to the living room. He tried to calm his nerves and rid his mind of the sarcasm he felt.

"Let me start again," he finally said as Laurelin fashionably rearranged herself on the sofa.

"What's to start?" Laurelin asked, appearing rather bored. "He's dead, and you've taken care of business there. Now I hope you'll take care of business here. I mean, really, Darrin. You've never mentioned the man except in the past tense, and now you're acting as though you've just gone through some tremendously difficult circumstance. How could it be that traumatic if you wrote him off so many years ago anyway?"

Darrin found her attitude not only distasteful, but downright aggravating. His desire to keep from arguing was rapidly disappearing.

"I'm sorry, dear. I'm sure this is difficult for you to deal with, but you must know that your vast mercy is misplaced on such a man as my father." His voice dripped sarcasm, and he rolled up his shirt sleeves like a man preparing to do battle.

"My father is, or rather was, an alcoholic. He and my mother were separated because she refused to let her only son be raised by the bottle. I grew up hating my father for what he had done. However, after my mother died, I was the one the police would come to after every drunk driving arrest and every accident. I've let you assume he was already dead because in many ways—all the ways that mattered—he was. It was wrong of me to lead you on about it, but I was naturally very disturbed and ashamed of the man. I wanted nothing more to do with him, yet it was only right that upon his death, the police would call me."

"But you hated him, right?" she asked with a tiny shake of her head. "So, it's not like this is a tug at any emotional heart-strings, right?"

Darrin had fixed his gaze upon her, but it was as if he could no longer see her. His mind seemed to play tricks on him. He could hear her voice, but all he could think of were the Heywards.

"So what's the big deal, Darrin? He's dead, and now you don't have to worry about him bothering you or us ever again. I don't see where this is really a problem. It's not like you or he loved each other or had this binding father-son relationship. He was a drunken fool, and you are better off without him. Now if that's all, can we *please* talk about the wedding?" Laurelin crossed her legs in the opposite direction and waited for Darrin's usual surrender.

Her words snapped him back to reality. "Laurelin, you never cease to amaze me. Were you born this calloused and cynical, or did you have to work up to it? I just can't understand you. You know nothing about my father except for what I have just told you. Granted, I abhorred the man, but at least I have *reasons.* You only hate him because his death managed to cut into your agenda by taking me to Dallas for two days. Time, which I might add, could have been used to your benefit, if you had chosen to act like a grown-up instead of a spoiled little girl."

He was letting his anger out, and he could tell by the look of feigned surprise that Laurelin was taking particular delight in his losing control. Instead of letting her respond, he continued as he ripped away the tie at his neck. "So, in answer to your question, no, we *cannot* talk about the wedding now, because *I* was not finished explaining the situation to you."

He tossed the tie across the chair and went into the kitchen for a glass of something cold. Finding a can of cola, he popped the top and took a long, steady drink. This wasn't how he wanted things to be. He needed comfort right now. He needed to find a reason to believe that things would get better. He needed. . .What did he need?

"Turn it over to God" he could almost hear his mother saying.

Oh, God, help me, he prayed and took another drink. He was surprised and grateful that Laurelin hadn't followed him into the kitchen or called out to him. Slowly he took a deep breath and walked back into the living room.

"Look, I don't want to fight with you tonight. I don't want to plan a wedding, and I don't want to listen to any complaints about my absence. Yes, my father is dead because of his own stupidity, and yes, in its own way, it is a blessing. However, my father's stupidity has also cost the lives of two other individuals. This is an important thing."

"But the crash was in Texas. That's why you had to fly to Dallas, right?"

Darrin nodded curtly and took another drink.

"So *why* is it so important? We don't know the other people, and they didn't know us. None of our friends will find out about this, if that's what's bothering you. Just keep quiet about it."

Darrin shook his head in disbelief. Who *was* this woman before him? Had she always been this way? Had he really loved her at one point and time? He knew for certain he harbored no such feelings now, and he longed to tell her so—but it wasn't the right time.

"Laurelin, the couple he killed was from Lawrence. Do you know where that is?"

"Oh, Larryville?" she said, throwing out the insulting nickname. "The one in Kansas? That little college town, right?"

"Yes, that's the one. I met their daughter on the flight down to Dallas."

"You didn't tell her did you? She doesn't know it was your father, does she?"

"No, I didn't realize how the situations were connected until I saw the pictures of her parents and my father on the evening news. She told me her parents were killed in a car accident and that she was headed to Dallas, but I figured Dallas is a big city and—"

"She isn't going to sue your father's estate is she? Is this what you've been trying to tell me all evening? Oh, this *does* change everything. I wonder. . ."

Darrin had taken more than he could deal with. Going to the front door, he opened it and motioned to her. "Just get out. Go back to your perfectly decorated apartment and wonder about it there. I can't deal with you. I don't want to deal with you. Go decorate something for someone, but don't come near me. I don't want to hear from you or see you. You disgust me. Two innocent people lost their lives, and all you care to ask me is if their bereaved daughter is going to sue. Well, whether she sues or not, I am going to help her and her remaining family in any way I possibly can. That means financially, emotionally, or whatever other way they need assistance."

Laurelin winced but still hadn't bothered to get up from the sofa. "You're going to give them money? Darrin, why? That's just asking for a lawsuit of major proportions. Look, I have a great lawyer who can tell you exactly how to handle this. Just don't do anything stupid. If you go telling this woman who you are and give her money, well, who knows what will happen? You'll probably find the whole thing on the front page of the paper.

"Darrin, you need to be responsible about this. Think of our wedding—our friends. Think about the shop and your clientele. You can't risk this getting out. I don't want *anyone* to know about it. You haven't spoken to your father for years. Don't bring him home now that he's a ghost. I don't know what I'd do if any of our friends found out, Darrin. I really don't."

"Out!" Darrin's face flushed and his heartbeat quickened. What made him think he could ever live in the same world, let alone the same house, with this woman?

Laurelin smiled coyly and walked ever-so-gracefully to the door. "Fine, Darrin. You play it your way. You're just upset, but once you calm down you'll see that I'm right."

She took up her purse and came to stop in front of him. "You just might want to think about one thing. What makes you believe that once she discovers that it was your daddy who killed her parents, she'll want anything to do with you? Or worse yet, what if the pittance you offer her isn't enough and she keeps milking this thing for years? You'll want me then. You'll need someone like me to get you out of your self-imposed nightmare. I just hope you realize it before it's too late and you've given all your assets to those hicks in Lawrence."

She reached a hand up to touch his chest. "Look, Darrin, I'm not being cruel. I'm just being realistic. You can't change anything by wallowing in self-pity and anguish over what your father did. You're nothing like him, and you don't need to attach yourself to his wrongdoings. You're like me. We're survivors. More still, we're victors."

Darrin took hold of her hand and removed it from his chest. "Lin, please just go before I say something we're both going to regret."

Laurelin shrugged. "Have it your way. But just remember, we're engaged, and your assets are important to me."

"I thought I was important to you," he said.

Laurelin smiled coquettishly. "Well, of course. That goes without saying."

"It seems a lot of truly important things go without saying," Darrin replied. He came very close to concluding their conversation by breaking their engagement, but something held him back. "Just give me some time, Lin, okay? I'll call you when

I'm ready to talk about all of this."

"Well, just so long as you don't take too long," Laurelin replied. "I can't put a wedding together overnight."

As usual, she had the last word and slipped out the door before Darrin could even register a proper comment. Everything that came to mind had to do with telling her that they could take all the time they wanted, because there wasn't going to be a wedding.

seven

"Excuse me, can I get a double espresso to go?" a harried woman asked while juggling a stack of books and papers.

Leslie's head began to spin. She'd been at Crossroads for almost nine hours straight, and because it was only two blocks from the University of Kansas, the shop was nearly always packed. It was nearing midnight, and the college students were preparing for all-nighters with last minute to-go orders of double everythings, except decaffeinated anything.

She smiled at the woman. "Sure thing."

Quickly, she made her way back to the wooden counter. She filled the large paper cup with the steaming liquid and applied the lid. She mechanically punched in the price on the cash register, derived the total, and delivered the goods to the book-laden woman. "That'll be $2.58." Leslie waited while the woman rummaged around in an ancient-looking billfold.

"Here you go." She handed Leslie a five-dollar bill. "Keep it. You look like you could use a double espresso yourself." She smiled and picked up some papers that had escaped her. "Have a good night," she called over her shoulder on the way out of the shop.

"Yeah," Leslie muttered and sighed deeply. Looking around, she suddenly realized she was all alone. *Good,* she thought, glancing at her watch. *I can close early tonight.* She dragged her exhausted body over to the entrance and locked the door. She flipped the sign to SORRY, WE'RE CLOSED! and began clearing any tables she'd overlooked throughout the night.

After thirty minutes of cleaning, Leslie was more than ready to leave, yet she still had to count the money in the drawer and balance it against the receipts. That would consume as much as an hour of her time. "At least Margie's got the store in the morning," she breathed with relief.

Carefully she entered each receipt into the adding machine as her parents had taught her to do so many years ago. How old had she been? Eight? Nine? She smiled at the bittersweet memories of her patient mother, who never became frustrated or angry when Leslie failed to remember to push the plus button or lost count of the daily earnings.

Leslie reflected fondly on the first time she "took the drawer down," as her father called it, all by herself. Her parents had beamed with pride, despite the fact that they'd helped the gangly, blond pony-tailed girl every step of the way. They always knew how to build up her confidence and make her feel as though the world were at her fingertips.

"Oh, Mama, Daddy. I still need you so much!" Tears caught in her long lashes and spilled onto the stacks of papers and currency. "This is so hard without you. I'm so tired, and I know Aunt Margie is, too, but we're trying. We want to keep the store, and goodness knows we need to. I haven't even gone down to the basement to find your box of papers!"

Leslie thought about the shoe box full of deeds, wills, receipts, and other important documents. Her parents never forgot to remind her about the box before leaving on a trip. It was a part of the routine. And for the longest time, she hadn't thought anything of it. Nothing would ever come of it anyhow, she'd convinced herself over the years. She'd never need to go find the box and deal with its confidential contents.

The tears fell harder now. She recalled the first time the seriousness of their instructions had finally caught up with her. *What if something did happen?* she remembered thinking. *I'm only eighteen years old. What if they die and I suddenly have to handle everything alone?* But just as quickly, she'd brushed aside her worries. Nothing was going to happen to her parents.

How often did things like that occur? No, her parents were strong and healthy and very cautious people. They'd no doubt live to a ripe old age, and she'd not have to deal with "the box" until she was an old woman with kids of her own.

Leslie smiled briefly, reflecting on the naive reasoning of her youth. "I'm twenty-four, and I still don't know what to do. Everything was supposed to be so clear by now, but it's still as hazy as it was when I was a teenager! And I still can't believe that they're gone. Just like that. One minute here—the next in heaven."

But she had to believe it. As often was the case, the truth was a hard pill to swallow. It was time for her to be responsible. It was time to locate the sacred box. The box that summarized her parents' lives and that would forever change hers. She tried to mentally unearth it from the myriad of clothes and old toys her mother had stored in the basement. Perhaps it was beside the rocking horse. Yes, she seemed to recall seeing the large, brown shoebox wrapped tightly in rubber bands and sealed securely in a clear plastic bag. She would definitely have to look when she returned home.

Wiping the tears from her eyes, she walked to the women's bathroom to splash cold water on her face. The place was a mess, as usual. Paper towels had overflown the trash container and now lay strewn around the small room. One more job to do before she could go home.

When both restrooms were set in order, Leslie carried out the last of the trash and heaved it into the bin with a groan.

"Finally!" she sighed, locking the back door. She gathered up her purse and jacket and gave the shop one last lookover. Satisfied, she made her way to her parked Toyota and wearily drove home.

❧

"Hello?" Leslie called as she unlocked the front door of her house.

"In here," Margie's voice emanated from the kitchen. Leslie found her, nightgown-clad, her face wan. In her hands was a china cup with what appeared to be tea. No doubt it was a cup of Margie's favorite chamomile. "How was your day?" Margie asked.

"Long. Too long. But everything's balanced and ready for your morning arrival, Auntie dear." A weak smile played at her lips. "Tips were decent." Margie nodded approvingly, and Leslie continued. "So how was Travis?"

Margie shifted uncomfortably in her chair. "Well, Les, I don't know what to do with him. He's so quiet. Too quiet. You've seen him. He just sits in his room or on the couch. Doesn't even care if cartoons are the show *du jour* or not. I'd be lying if I told you I wasn't worried."

Leslie nodded sadly, knowing full well the extent of the little boy's sorrow. "I am, too, Margie. Maybe tomorrow I'll call Pastor Parkinson. He may have some ideas, because I'm sure out of them. I mean, I knew this would be hard for Travis to deal with, but I never thought he'd just withdraw altogether. I guess I expected him to cry a lot and be clingy. I think I could have handled that, but this is. . .well. . .it just doesn't seem natural."

"I know. This is just so very hard." Rising to her feet, Margie walked to her niece and embraced her.

Leslie felt as though the older woman were trying to draw energy and momentum from her body, but unfortunately, she had none left to offer. Her aunt was dipping into a dry well.

Margie drew away and yawned. "Well, I guess I'm off to bed. Morning will come around awfully quick as it is."

Leslie nodded. "You know, you don't have to wait up for me. I'm a big girl now and I. . ." She could see a flicker of hurt in her aunt's expression. "Oh, pay me no attention. I'm so tired I don't know if I'm coming or going. I'm going to go take a hot shower and go to bed." She gave Margie a peck on the cheek. "Thanks for caring about me."

"That's what I'm here for," the older woman replied.

Leslie found some comfort in her words. "I'll probably see you before you leave in the morning. Even if he is the picture of dejection, Travis's internal alarm clock is perpetually set at 7:30." Both emitted a strained laugh, and Margie began to walk toward the guest room. Before she was out of sight, Leslie spoke again. "I'm really glad you're here, Margie. I mean that. I don't think I could live in this house without your help and support."

The woman turned and offered a weak smile. "I know what you mean, Les. I don't think I could be alone, either." With that, she disappeared into the darkness of the doorway.

Leslie made her way to the spacious bathroom and turned the nozzles until she had the desired temperature. Steam rose to meet her face, and she inhaled deeply. This working arrangement would, no doubt, be the death of her. She felt so old. She and Margie traded time at the shop. Margie took days so that Leslie could spend more waking hours with Travis. Leslie was more in tune with the night crowd anyway. She'd always show up around four in the afternoon, bringing Travis in tow, and she and Margie would exchange shop and child, like couriers bent on a secret mission. It seemed the easiest answer, and for six days out of the week, this was to be the routine.

Sundays had always been set aside for family, and the shop was closed, much to the grumbling of the clientele. Leslie cherished Sundays. They made it a true day of rest, usually characterized by naps after morning church service and lunch. Sometimes the afternoon lent itself to trips to the park or the museum. In the past they'd even taken day trips to Kansas City or Topeka. Leslie fondly remembered those times she'd gone along when her parents had planned some special outing for Travis.

Poor Travis.

The once vivacious boy was not dealing well with the absence of his parents, and often did nothing but surrender to fitful sleep. Leslie had tried to find books that dealt with childhood trauma and how to help children cope with losing their parents, but the pickings were very slim. Christian books often fell short of really offering anything solid for children.

She didn't know how to comfort her brother, and that seemed the most important thing right now. Nothing either woman did would console the child. It was as though his entire five-year-old being was drenched in anguish. His eyes looked hollow, and his appetite had greatly diminished. His ashen face and the ever-present dreamy look in his blue eyes broke Leslie's heart each time she saw him.

As the massaging jets of the showerhead stripped away the trials and worries of the day, Leslie tried to focus on ways to help her baby brother. She could think of nothing at all, save counseling. Professional and educated counseling. There was a great hospice organization in Topeka. Someone at church had mentioned being helped by a warm teddy bear of a man named Byron. It seemed he worked at the hospice and dealt primarily with children. It was at least worth considering. Someone had to be able to reach Travis. Somehow, he would work through this. He just had to. Leslie realized that without him, she really had nothing left of her parents, or herself.

Reluctantly, she turned the water off and stepped onto the terry cloth mat beside the tub. Slipping into her fuzzy, mulberry-colored robe, she lightly towel-dried her hair and made her way down the hall to Travis's room. She peaked her head through the cracked door and watched as he slumbered. All at once, his mouth contorted slightly, his brow wrinkled, and he tossed and turned violently. Then, he snuggled back into his covers and tightly clenched his teddy bear.

Tears sprang to Leslie's eyes once more. "Dear God, please

give him peace. He's only a little guy." She thought of how they'd all called him their "Baby Guy" when he'd been born. He was tiny and feisty and so unique to the Heyward household.

"God, he can't deal with this alone. I can't deal with this alone, either, and I don't know how to comfort him when I can't even comfort myself. I know there has to be an answer. Maybe it's just that we all need time, but I love him so much," she whispered through her stifled sobs. "Please, Lord, give me back my Baby Guy."

Gingerly, she stepped into Travis's room. It was typical little boy motif, filled with building blocks, stuffed animals, and all the latest science fiction collectibles. Leslie mourned that the toys had not been played with for some time. Approaching his bedside, she eased onto her knees and looked into the troubled face of her brother. He was her entire life now. Nothing else mattered. Not the shop, not herself, not anything in this world. She loved him with her entire being. Just when she thought she had reached her limit and could no longer go on, the thought of Travis urged her forward. It was a feeling she had never thought possible.

Of course, she had loved him when her parents were still alive. But this was so much more intense. Every time she looked at him, her heart leaped into her throat, and she was forced to choke back sobs of joy, of frustration, of love. He was truly the only thing that made her remember she was alive.

Leaning closer, she softly kissed his flushed cheek. He stirred a bit and then seemed to relax. "Good night, my angel. Sissy promises to help you get better." Tears plopped onto his comforter, and Leslie inhaled a ragged breath. "I promise." Rising, she tiptoed back and noiselessly closed the door.

She leaned against the wall for a moment and sighed. There was nothing she could do. Nothing in her power would make him better. But God's power was another story. She might be helpless, but He wasn't. She had to believe that God could work through all the details.

"Just show me what to do, God," she prayed, and instantly an image of the shoebox came to mind. It was time to deal with the facts of the situation. Desperate for sleep but compelled to seek out the box, Leslie put aside her desires for bed and instead went to the basement.

☙

Darrin found his mind consumed with thoughts of Leslie, and when he could no longer restrain himself from action, he got in the car and drove to Lawrence. A quaint little town with hilly, winding streets, Lawrence had a village-style atmosphere in its downtown district. There were marvelous Victorian homes that lined narrow lanes, as well as completely modern housing architecture. Darrin found it peaceful and stimulating at the same time.

He drove down Massachusetts, the main drag through town, and turned off at Fourteenth Street. He rechecked the address one more time and headed up the steep hill that led toward the college campus. Then without warning he saw it. The large wooden sign with antique lettering: Crossroads.

He felt his chest tighten, and he pulled the car into the only available parking spot, nearly half a block away. For a moment, he just sat, staring at the shop. There were two shops really. One was Crossroads; the other was a small mom-n-pop drugstore that sported a sign in the window that read WINTER SALE. The building the two businesses shared was quaint, like the neighborhood, and seemed to have a generous number of patrons coming and going. That helped him relax a bit. Perhaps he could just slip in and out unnoticed and get a feel for the welfare of Leslie Heyward.

He approached the shop amid an onslaught of chattering girls. He waited until they'd passed into the shop before trying to follow them. Inside, the darkness instantly demanded his eyes adjust, and when they did, he found Leslie behind the counter taking orders from the talkative group.

Standing back, he just watched for several minutes. He was clearly out of place with all the young college students, but no one seemed to pay him much attention. Perhaps they thought he was a professor or instructor from the college. Perhaps they didn't care who he was. Everyone seemed quite wrapped up in their own world, and even as one table of customers seemed to rise in unison and move toward the exit, no one appeared to care that he stood idle in the middle of the room.

The girls took their coffee and rushed past him, giggling about something that one of the group had said. He watched them for a moment, then noticed that Leslie was watching him. *Did she remember him from the plane?* he wondered.

He smiled. "I don't remember being that young," he told her as he approached the counter.

A wistful look engulfed Leslie's face. "I do. And how I wish I could go back." Quickly, her expression melted into a customer-friendly grin, and she wiped away puddles of spilt coffee from the counter. She lifted her eyes to meet his face, those brilliant blue-green eyes he remembered so well. "So, what'll it be?"

Darrin breathed a sigh of relief. Apparently she didn't remember him, or if she did, she wasn't acknowledging it. "I don't know. I've never been here before. What do you suggest?"

"Well, it depends on what you like. If you're looking to stay awake all night, I'd suggest a double espresso with your favorite flavoring. If you're looking for something to warm you up from the cold, but don't want the caffeine, I'd suggest a decaf latte."

"What do you like?" he asked, taking a stool at the counter.

Leslie looked up for a moment. "I'm particularly fond of the grand-sized latte with raspberry."

"Does that come in decaf? I don't think I want to be up all

night," Darrin said with a quick glance around the room. The place was nearly deserted, and he suddenly felt quite conscious of the fact.

"You can have it in decaf," Leslie told him and picked up a mug. "Is that what you'd like?"

"Sure. I'll give it a try."

"Is that for here or to go?"

"Here."

She smiled and went to work, bringing back a glass mug of rose-tinted liquid. "I hope you like it." As she handed it to him, her face assumed a look of concern. "I'd feel pretty bad if I suggested it and you turned out hating it."

Darrin took a taste and nodded. "It's good. Never thought about raspberry coffee before."

"We get all kinds here," Leslie said, busying herself with odd jobs behind the counter. "The kids can come up with some really crazy combinations."

"Kids? You don't look like much more than a kid yourself."

"Oh, aren't you the charmer?"

"I suppose you get a lot of those, too," he said, taking another drink.

Leslie laughed. "Yeah, like I said, we get all kinds."

"But seriously," Darrin began, "don't you go to the university?"

"No. I'm the owner of this shop. I graduated from there some time ago, and now I spend all my time here. Or so it seems. My name is Leslie Heyward."

"I'm Darrin," he offered, deciding against giving his last name in case she made the connection. "Well, it looks like a great place. I'll have to remember it."

"We'd love to have you back."

The small talk seemed to wear on his nerves, and yet he was drawn to the petite blond in the same way he had been on the plane. "So, when you're not here, what do you do?"

"Mostly I spend time at home with Travis. He consumes a lot of my time, especially now." The telephone rang and Leslie excused herself.

Travis? Darrin couldn't help but wonder who Travis might be. Would it be rude to come right out and ask? He sipped at the coffee and waited for her to return. But when Leslie hung up the phone, she grabbed a tray and went out to clean tables. Darrin had no choice but to turn around if he wanted to talk with her or ignore her and act like a regular customer whose attention was on coffee and not the proprietor. His heart won over and he twisted around on the stool.

"So, you were telling me about your off hours."

Leslie kept her back to him and continued wiping at the table. "I don't have many of them, but like I said, they're usually consumed with about a million things. My parents recently died—in fact, the funeral was just a few days ago. It's about all I can do to keep up."

Darrin was glad she couldn't see his expression because he was certain he had grimaced. "I'm sorry about your folks."

"Yeah, me too. It's been especially hard on Travis."

"Who's that—a boyfriend?" There, the question was finally asked.

Leslie laughed. "No. I don't have a boyfriend. When would I find the time?"

Darrin found himself relieved at her answer and, for reasons beyond his understanding, almost smiled. But her next words put aside such joyous thoughts.

"Travis is my little brother. He's only five. Guess you could say he was one of those late-life or at least mid-life surprises for my folks." She turned and straightened, the glass-ladened tray balanced expertly in her hand. "Travis isn't dealing very well with this at all. He's not talking much these days, and it's becoming pretty evident that he's going to need some professional help to get through losing his mom and dad."

Darrin felt instantly sickened. A child! A little boy named Travis was now without his parents because Darrin's own father had. . .It was too much to even consider. Why was it suddenly so much worse than before? It wasn't like he didn't know that people were affected by the Heywards' deaths, but he'd never for one moment envisioned that a child would be orphaned by the accident.

"I'm so sorry. How horrible for a little boy to be confronted with the death of his parents. I suppose you were left as his guardian?"

She nodded. "Mom and Dad had the good sense to plan it all out with a will, but I would have cared for him anyway. We're terribly close."

"I suppose something like this is never really planned for."

"No, not really, but Mom and Dad did their best to make it easy on us. They had one of those prearranged funeral plans." She smiled rather sheepishly. "I could have saved myself a great deal of worry if I'd just bothered to go through their private papers first thing. I don't know why I put it off. I guess going through those papers made their deaths more real—more final."

"I can understand that," he replied sympathetically. "So everything was arranged and taken care of, and you only had to worry about seeing that their wishes were carried out?"

"Pretty much so. Wish it could be that easy for Travis. When you're five, death has very little meaning."

"But when you're an adult watching a child deal with death, it has a great deal of meaning."

He could see Leslie's eyes sparkle with tears. "Yeah, it's really hard to watch him deteriorate like this. I love him so much. Everybody does. He's so good-natured—or at least he was. It's just not fair." As if embarrassed for her muted outburst, she offered a pain-filled smile. "Sometimes I'm not very understanding when it comes to trusting God to work this out for the best."

"I completely understand. I have my fair share of questions to ask Him. And that's on a good day!" Darrin removed a five-dollar bill from a monogrammed wallet and handed it to Leslie. She began to fumble for change in the pocket of her apron, but Darrin reached out and placed his hand on her forearm. "No, you go ahead and keep that."

He got to his feet and drained the rest of the coffee. "Thanks a lot. I really enjoyed this place."

"I'm glad. Thank *you* for listening to me. I don't seem to be getting much contact with the outside world, except for my aunt. Between our hours here and watching Travis, we don't have much time for heart-to-heart conversations." Clearing Darrin's mug from the counter and wiping the pinewood with a damp cloth, Leslie turned to face him. "Do come back."

Darrin smiled. "I plan on it. See you later."

As soon as he was out-of-doors, Darrin heaved a sigh. He felt like a wound had not only reopened, but that it had become deeper. Leslie *and* her little brother were suffering from the sins of his father. A five-year-old child was left with only an overworked, overworried sister and an aunt to care for him. A twenty-four-year-old woman was left with a business, a grieving brother, and no additional guidance. And he was left with the guilt. The guilt of knowing that, had it not been for the irresponsible acts of Michael Malone, they would be a very happy and complete family.

eight

As the weeks blended together, Leslie found herself growing more and more weary of everything. She was sick of the shop and the routine there. She was tired of dealing with problems that she had no answers for and had reached an absolute limit with Travis.

In the weeks since their parents' accident, Travis had gone through a period of silence and distancing. He chose to stay in his room for hours on end, and even when Leslie tried to draw him out, he would refuse. It was a real trial to take him to church or the park or anywhere else for that matter. But during the last week he'd passed into another stage of mourning. His security level plummeted, and he demanded to have Leslie's utmost attention at every turn. He cried every time she left him, and whenever she'd return to the house, he'd cling to her for hours. This happened even when she was working late at night, and it worried her more than she could say.

She'd fully intended to seek some counseling for him, but her pastor didn't think it would require anything so professional or detailed, at least not at this point. He suggested she just give the boy time and let nature run its course. But as far as Leslie was concerned, nature's course was beginning to frighten her.

The Saturday evening crowd finally thinned out and eventually left the shop. Leslie was exhausted, partially because of being on her feet since late afternoon, and partially because Travis's nightmares often kept them both awake at night and she wasn't getting much sleep. Leslie cleaned up, counted the money, and headed for her car. She was too tired to think and knew that she shouldn't be driving, but the trip home was short and she tried to focus all her attention on the steep hill that was Fourteenth Street. She breathed a sigh of relief to find it clear of snow and ice, but nevertheless slipped the car into low gear to save wear on her brakes.

Just as she crossed the intersection at Kentucky Street, Leslie had the scare of her life. Out of nowhere a car came barreling down the street, and before Leslie could clear the intersection, it clipped the back end of her Toyota and spun her around.

"Great!" she exclaimed as she came to a stop. "This is just what I need." The shock of the accident kept her foot firmly on the brake and her hands on the wheel for several long minutes.

The driver from the other vehicle had run a red light and, after hitting Leslie, had run the front end of his car up on the sidewalk. There it sat, precariously balanced half on and half off the street. For a second, Leslie took a mental inventory. She felt all right and didn't think any real injury had come to her from the accident.

The car—well, that would take getting out to survey the damage, and since it was after midnight, Leslie was hesitant to do so. She'd just read how people were sometimes rear-ended or run into in order for the driver of the other vehicle to do further harm to the occupants of the incapacitated car. But no one in the other vehicle seemed inclined to get out and check on her. Maybe they were hurt. Maybe she should go to them and stop worrying about the consequences.

She sat there wondering what she should do, when to her relief the flashing lights of a Lawrence police car came into view behind her. "Thank you, Father," she whispered as she turned off her engine.

The police car was soon joined by another. Leslie gave her statement, trying to remember every detail. She was amazed at how much she took for granted. How fast was she going? Was the light green or had it already turned amber when she went through? Was she wearing her seat belt? Had there been any ice on the roadway?

She tried to make certain of her answers. The seat belt situation was easy—she always wore it and demanded that anyone riding in her car wear theirs as well. Aunt Margie often protested, saying that they never worried about such things when she was a child, but nevertheless she'd wear one for Leslie. She gave the answers that she thought were correct. She was certain that she wasn't going over the speed limit because she always geared down to come down the hill and she hadn't yet geared back up when she'd been hit.

The officer was noting everything, and it was while he was finishing that she noted the other driver was led away in handcuffs. His loud protests left Leslie little doubt as to his sobriety.

"It doesn't look like there's much damage here," the officer told her. "In fact, you were very lucky."

"It wasn't luck," Leslie replied, her breath coming out in puffs of steam against the cold February night. "I'm sure God was watching out for me."

The officer seemed unimpressed with her faith and, after finishing his report, gave her a copy of the insurance information from the other driver and offered to follow her to her house in order to make sure the car could operate properly. Leslie thanked him and headed the car in the direction of home. She had just reached down to turn up the heater when she noted that the dashboard clock read 1:35.

"Oh, Margie will be sick with worry," she exclaimed.

Ten minutes later she pulled into her driveway and waved to the police officer as she made her way to the house. Margie was waiting for her with a fearful expression on her face.

"Where have you been? I called the shop, but you were already gone."

"Oh, I know, and I'm so sorry. I was coming down Fourteenth when a drunk driver hit my car. He barely clipped the backside, so the damage is real limited, but it scared me. Coming home just now, I thought of Mom and Dad and how they didn't fare as well from their drunk driver."

Margie nodded. "People are so thoughtless to drink themselves into a stupor and then get behind the wheel of a car. Even if it wasn't illegal, they ought not to take people's lives into their own hands."

"Well, I'll have to call the insurance agent tomorrow. Do you think I can get ahold of him on Sunday?"

"It's hard to say, but I'd imagine there's some kind of emergency number. How do you feel? You weren't hurt were you? Whiplash sometimes doesn't show up right away."

Leslie rubbed her neck. "No, I don't think I'm hurt."

At this, both women were startled to find Travis screaming Leslie's name as he ran down the stairs. "Leslie! You're hurt!"

"No," Leslie said, lifting him in her arms. He wrapped his arms so tightly around Leslie's neck that she was nearly deprived of air. "Trav, stop squeezing so tight," she gasped and pried his arms away. "Travis, I'm okay. I had a little accident tonight, but I'm okay. God was taking good care of me."

Travis sobbed hysterically, and it was an hour before Leslie and Margie could get him calm. Leslie finally decided to let him sleep in her bed that night, even though she questioned the sensibility of it. What if he decided he needed to sleep with her every night? That would certainly never do.

She carried him upstairs, talking soothingly all the way, while Margie followed behind, snapping off lights. "Tomorrow," she told Travis, "we'll go to church and then maybe we can. . ."

"I don't want to ride in the car. The car will kill me," Travis told her adamantly. "The car killed Mommy and Daddy."

Leslie exchanged glances with Margie before answering. "No, sweetie, it wasn't the car's fault. It was the fault of the person driving the car. Remember, I told you. The man had too much alcohol to drink, and he didn't know what he was doing. He shouldn't have been driving. Just like the man tonight. He shouldn't have been driving, but because he didn't think about the consequences, he did what he wanted to anyway. Now I'm all right, and we need to get some sleep, so I want you to just stop worrying about it. Okay?"

Travis nodded sleepily but said nothing. Leslie shook her head at Margie's mournful expression and took Travis into her room. It was going to be a long night.

❧

"But Travis, I thought you understood. Remember what I told you about the car? It can't hurt anybody by itself. We're just driving to church and back. We won't be hurt, I promise." But even as the words were out of her mouth, Leslie wondered how she would ever explain it, if by some strange twist of fate, they were in another accident.

Travis had planted himself under the bed and refused to come out. Even now, as Leslie lay on her stomach and tried to coax him from his hiding place, she could see that her pleas were having little effect. He was terrified, and there was no way he was going to climb into a car again without a great deal of thought and possibly professional help.

"Come on, Trav, I'll take good care of us."

"No!" He scooted further back toward the headboard end of the bed.

Leslie sighed and glanced up at Margie, who waited in anxious worry by the door. "Margie, you go on to church. I don't think we'll be going today, but maybe you could have everyone pray for us."

Margie grimaced. "Are you sure you don't want me to stay here with you?"

"No, we'll be fine. Travis and I just need to spend some time together."

Margie left in silence, and for several minutes Leslie just lay with her cheek against the hardwood floor of Travis's room. Travis watched her without moving. The terror in his eyes made Leslie feel terrible. She felt like it was all her fault. If she'd only been more cautious telling Margie about the accident, Travis might never have heard. On the other hand, it was probably only a matter of time until his fears had taken over anyway. Better to deal with it now, she guessed.

"Hey, Trav, I know what we could do."

"What?" he asked softly.

"Well, it snowed again last night, and I was thinking maybe we could make a snowman in the yard."

"You won't make me ride in the car?"

"No," she answered. "I love you, baby. I don't want you to be afraid."

He started to cry. "I miss Mommy and Daddy."

Tears formed in Leslie's eyes. "I miss them, too. Say, would you like to walk over to the cemetery?"

"So we can see them?" Travis asked, sounding almost hopeful.

"Well, they aren't there, not really. You remember what I told you about them being in heaven, don't you?"

"You said they just left their bodies here."

"That's right." Leslie's back began to ache, so she sat up, thinking that perhaps Travis would at least come to the edge of the bed in order to better talk to her. "It's like your box of toys. You have the outside box, but the real treasure is the toys inside. Mommy and Daddy had bodies that were kind of like boxes to hold their spirits. Their spirits are the very best part, and that part has gone to heaven to live with Jesus."

Travis came out from under the bed and surprised Leslie by plopping down on her lap. "Do their spirits remember me?" he asked.

"I'm sure they do. You know, there's a lot about heaven that I don't understand or know much about, but I do know that people in heaven are never sad."

"Never? What if they fall down and get hurt?"

"You can't get hurt in heaven—there are no tears in heaven."

"Then let's go now, Sissy. I want to be in heaven with Mommy and Daddy."

Leslie hugged her brother close. Tears were streaming down her face. "Oh, baby, I want to be with them, too. I want to be with Jesus and never cry again, but it isn't time for us to go. When it's time, Jesus will come and get us, but until then, I need you here with me. I need someone to stay and help me be strong."

Travis looked up to see her tears. His lip quivered and puckered as he started to cry. Leslie reached out to wipe his tears. "We're going to make it through this, Travis. It hurts a lot right now, but it won't hurt this bad forever. We need to let God help us, though. In the Bible, God says that He loves us and that He'll be with us even when we're afraid."

"I'm 'fraid, Sissy," Travis said, snuggling against her.

Leslie nodded. "I know you are. Sometimes, I'm afraid, too. But you know what? I remember a little verse in the Bible, and it helps me to know that I'm going to be all right."

"What is it?" he asked, his breath ragged.

"Psalm 56:3," Leslie replied. "'When I am afraid, I will trust in You.'"

"When I'm 'fraid, I'll trust in You," Travis whispered.

"Can you remember that?" Leslie asked him softly.

Travis nodded, and Leslie smiled. She only hoped she could do as well to remember it when fearful times were upon her.

nine

Darrin waited uncomfortably for Laurelin to show up at the apartment. He'd invited her to share dinner with him, with the determined purpose of telling her that it was over between them. The problem was, he didn't know how exactly he was going to handle the situation. Laurelin wasn't going to take rejection lightly, and there was no way she would see this as anything but rejection.

A bigger problem was that Laurelin was a great help with the store, and with several spring trips to Europe on his agenda, Darrin wasn't yet ready to be rid of the helpfulness of an assistant, especially one as savvy as Laurelin. Still, he couldn't string her along just in order to have her help at the store. She might even surprise him and ask to stay on with Elysium. Stranger things had come from Laurelin in the past.

A light-handed knock sounded at the door, and Darrin instantly recognized it as belonging to Laurelin. He opened the door and found her decked out in her full-length, arctic fox coat.

"Thanks for coming," he said, opening the door wide. "Come on in."

"Well, I must say, I haven't enjoyed your silent treatment one bit," Laurelin said, throwing off the coat to reveal a stunning winter-white pantsuit. "Nor have I enjoyed being responsible for the store all by myself. Oh, Gerda was there part-time, but she was practically useless. I don't know why you keep her. And I don't know why you call me to come over on the coldest day of the year. I swear the temperature has to be somewhere below zero."

Darrin took the coat and draped it over the back of a chair as his fiancée droned on. Laurelin had berated him quite severely once for daring to hang her coat on a hanger in his closet. He really wasn't sure what proper etiquette required in caring for arctic fox. Personally, he thought the coat looked better on the animal than on Laurelin, but he hadn't purchased it, so it really wasn't his place to complain.

"So did you order out for us?" she questioned, sniffing the air as if to identify the aroma.

Darrin smiled as he thought perhaps she should have kept the coat on. She looked like some sort of animal, sniffing the air for scent of her prey.

"What's so funny?" she suddenly asked, and Darrin realized that he'd been caught.

"Nothing, Lin. I doubt you'd see it the same way I did."

"Well," she paused as if deciding to pursue what she felt must be an insult. Then just as quickly she dismissed her concern and swept back her brown hair in a fluid, graceful move. "So, what are we eating?"

"I fixed us stir-fry," he said with an apologetic shrug. "It's pretty tasty, if I do say so myself."

"I suppose it will have to do," Laurelin replied. "Unless, of course, you'd like to take me out. I know this great new restaurant down on the plaza."

"No, I'm not going out tonight."

"Fine." She seemed to pout for a moment, but as Darrin turned to lead the way to the dining room, she followed without hesitation.

"I'm sorry I haven't been good company of late. I'm sorry, too, that I haven't called much or kept up with the parties and such. I've had a lot on my mind and felt it unfair to burden you with it," Darrin said as he took a chair opposite her.

He dished up steaming rice and then added a generous ladle of vegetables to top this before handing the plate to Laurelin. She murmured thanks as he doubled the portion for himself and then paused thoughtfully. "If you don't mind," he said, "I'd like to pray."

"Pray? *Now?*" Laurelin asked in disbelief. "Whatever for?"

"Because I feel thankful, that's why," Darrin said and bowed his head. "Father, I thank You for this food and the blessings You've bestowed. I ask You to be with me now as I share this meal with Laurelin. I ask that we might better understand Your will in our lives. In Jesus' name, amen."

Laurelin was still sitting there watching him as she had been before he'd bowed in prayer. "What in the world was that all about?"

"It's about a great deal," Darrin said, mixing the vegetables with the rice. "You've always known that I was a Christian, although I do apologize for not being a very active one. I've suddenly come to realize how very important prayer is to me, and that God needs to play a more major role in my life."

"Is *that* why you asked me over?" Her voice betrayed a tone of disbelief.

"Not completely. There are a great many things we need to discuss."

"Don't I know it," she answered rather haughtily. "You leave me virtually on hold for weeks, making an appearance when it suited you, leaving the store in limbo. Not to mention——"

Darrin held up his hand. "Lin, I don't want to fight."

"Well, neither do I," she snapped back. "But I do want some explanations."

"And you deserve to have them," Darrin answered. "That's exactly why I wanted us to get together. But not if it means that we spend the time yelling at each other. I've let that kind of communication go on too long. We need to be able to talk in a civilized manner to each other. You know what I mean? With respect and——"

"Darrin," Laurelin interrupted, putting a hand to her head, "don't try to psychoanalyze my life. I have one therapist, and

I don't need another."

"I'm not trying to be your therapist. I am trying to explain, however, that I'm only coming to see the error of my ways in a great many areas."

Laurelin sat back and smiled smugly. "Well, why didn't you say so in the first place? If you've brought me here to apologize, by all means have at it."

"It isn't that I feel the need to apologize," Darrin said, feeling angry at her suggestion that he owed her something other than an explanation. He tried to calm his feelings, remembering the time he'd spent in prayer before Laurelin's arrival. "Look, Lin, I want you to understand that I've come to realize how much I've distanced myself from God. As a Christian, I know that I'm to continue my spiritual walk and growth, but I feel like the past few years have been spent taking a nap alongside the path rather than pursuing the journey."

"Whatever are you talking about? We've been seen in church nearly every Sunday. Well, at least most every Sunday until that dreadful Dallas fiasco. Speaking of which, has that woman slapped you with a lawsuit yet? Is that why you called me?"

"No, she's not suing me."

"Well, don't bet on it. I'd keep a good lawyer on retainer just the same." Laurelin dug into the food and nodded. "This isn't too bad, Darrin."

"Thank you," he answered, feeling his patience begin to wear thin. He opened his mouth to try once again to explain the need to allow God to direct his life, when Laurelin started off on her own agenda.

"You know, Darrin, I've been looking at houses, and I know you'd wanted to put it off until a year or two after we marry, but I think we ought to consider getting a place right away. I have found the most delightful house, in the perfect neighborhood. We can entertain and have brokers over and. . ."

"I'm not buying a house, Laurelin," he said flatly and went to the kitchen for the coffee pot.

"But Darrin, this place is so small, and the neighborhood is becoming so overrun with people of lower standards than ours. I think it would do your image good to relocate. I'd suggest we live in my place, but there is even less room than here, and I know we'd never be happy there."

"No, I'm sure we wouldn't," Darrin said. "Which brings me to my point."

"Look, Darrin, it wouldn't hurt you at all to consider my feelings in the matter. I want to feel proud of the place I live in. I want a home that I can entertain in and not be afraid that all the guests will be discussing my poor taste behind my back."

"Laurelin, we aren't buying a house."

She glared at him and slammed down her fork. "You simply don't care about me, do you? Is this some kind of male control issue? Because if it is, I'm not buying into it."

"And I'm not buying a house. It has nothing to do with control issues, but it has everything to do with us," Darrin replied.

"You just don't understand how important this is, do you?" She was clearly angry. "You give more consideration to a know-nothing family in Lawrence that you don't even know than you do to the woman you're supposed to marry. I don't understand you. I don't understand your lack of consideration."

"Oh, and you're the queen of consideration, yourself," Darrin countered. Once again she'd led him where he didn't want to go. How crafty she was at manipulating people into arguments.

"I don't have to take this from you, Darrin."

"You know, Lin, you're right. I'm feeling a bit angry now, and I'm going to go for a drive. When I get back, I hope you'll have the good sense to be gone."

"You can't just walk out on me like this," Lin said, getting to her feet and following Darrin into the living room.

"I can and I will," Darrin replied, pulling his coat out of the closet. "And this time, I'll have the last word."

❧

Leslie glanced up at the sound of the bells ringing on the front door. She smiled to herself as she recognized one of her regular customers. It was that nice man, David. . .no, Darrin something. She didn't know much about him except that he liked to sit at the counter and talk to her rather than take a table or join anyone else. She reached for a glass mug and began preparing a decaf raspberry latte, knowing by now that this was his usual request.

"Brrrr," he said, dusting a few snowflakes from his coat. "It's definitely winter out there."

"I see it's started to snow again," Leslie offered.

"Yes, but I don't think it's going to make anything of itself." He unzipped the coat and nodded. "I see you've learned to know me pretty well."

"I try to keep track of my regulars," Leslie said with a smile. "But if you have a taste for something different tonight, you certainly aren't obligated to this." She held up the steaming mug of coffee as if posing a question of acceptance.

"No, by all means, let me have at it. I'm half frozen." He took the coffee and downed half of it while Leslie rang up his sale.

Leslie caught the motion of another customer at the opposite end of the counter and, after putting Darrin's change down in front of him, went to see what the man wanted. It wasn't a hectic night, and for that Leslie was both grateful and concerned. The cold sometimes had the opposite desired effect, and rather than finding the shop filled with people demanding hot drinks, Leslie found that they all stayed home and refused to venture out into the frigid night.

"I need one more, only make this to go," the man said, after

Leslie asked how she could serve him. She filled a paper cup, secured the lid, and took his money, all while allowing herself brief glimpses at Darrin. She couldn't help wondering who he was and why he always came alone. She always tried to imagine the lives of her customers, and some of them, most of them, were pretty ease to peg. Like the man she was waiting on just now. He wasn't all that well known to her, but what she did know was that he lived only a block away and the coffee shop afforded him a quick get-away from his crowded apartment. She knew it was crowded because usually the man was accompanied by four other people, all who claimed residence in the same student rental as he did. She didn't know his name. Didn't really care to, and yet, she knew his face and what he liked to drink in the way of coffee. Seemed a small pittance of information to summarize a man's life by.

The man took off, leaving Leslie to clean the space he'd just vacated. She waved good-bye to three women who were also regulars from the college. All three were housemothers for different campus sororities, and all came in once a week like clockwork to discuss their problems and accomplishments. They each ordered a different type of coffee and always had cinnamon scones to accompany their chats. They always stayed about an hour and a half and always left her a two-dollar tip. You didn't get any more regular than that.

But Darrin, he was different, and Leslie couldn't quite peg him. He'd only been coming in for the last few weeks, but in that short time she'd really come to enjoy his visits. Whenever he came, he always sought her out and struck up a conversation. He always wanted to know how the shop was doing— how she was doing. He seemed, too, to genuinely care about the answers, and he was overwhelmingly generous. He always left her tips that were three and four times the price of his order. She'd started to argue with him once when he'd left her a twenty after ordering a two-dollar cup of coffee, but he told her that was his way, and he wouldn't be moved to change his mind.

"So, how's business?" he asked as she cleaned her way back to his spot at the counter.

"It's been better," Leslie admitted, throwing the cloth into a bucket of bleach water that resided under the counter.

Darrin's face was still touched with a rosy glow from the cold, and Leslie liked the way his bright blue eyes seemed to sparkle with enthusiasm for her company. He was a handsome man, she thought. Handsome and considerate. She wondered if he was attached to someone somewhere, but because he never mentioned anyone, Leslie allowed herself to believe he was a free agent.

Not that it really mattered. She wasn't looking for anyone at this point in her life. There was so much trouble at home that dating wasn't an option, and considering anything beyond the day-to-day trials only made her feel desperately alone and hopeless. She knew God was there for her, but at times she longed for *someone* to be there as well.

"You aren't listening to me, are you?" Darrin questioned.

Leslie felt her face flush. "Sorry. I've just got a lot on my mind."

"Like the shop being slow?"

"That, among other things," she admitted. "You want another?" she asked, noting that his mug was nearly empty.

"Sure, it's decaf, right?"

She nodded and went to work while Darrin questioned her about her week and why business was off. "Mostly it's because of the cold. You'd think cold weather would bring out the coffee and hot chocolate drinkers, but because most of the college kids are on foot, getting out in this cold doesn't hold near the attraction that staying home and fixing your own hot drinks has. I'm sure it will pick up in time." *At least I hope it does,* she added to herself.

"But that's not all you have on your mind, is it?"

Leslie bit at her lower lip before answering. "No, I guess it ranks down second or third on the list."

"What's number one?"

Leslie noted genuine concern in his expression. His eyes seemed to reflect unspoken questions, and his attention warmed her heart. "Travis," she finally murmured.

"Your little brother?"

"That'd be the one." She tried to sound lighthearted, but it was almost impossible. "He's having a lot of trouble with the death of our parents." She noted that Darrin visibly winced and quickly moved to change the subject. "But he'll be all right. What about you? Did you have a good work week?"

"What happened with me isn't important. Tell me about Travis. Are you getting him counseling?"

"Well, we didn't go that route at first. Our pastor was kind of the old-fashioned sort who figured kids in their resilient natures would bounce back from death in a fairly reasonable fashion. He told us to let nature run its course, but as time passed by and Travis started having more and more nightmares, I figured nature wasn't running the way it should. Now, Travis won't even get into the car without hysterical, traumatic fits, and, frankly, I'm worn out from dealing with it."

Darrin appeared compassionately interested, and Leslie found herself clinging to his attentiveness like a drowning woman. He was good for her. He was like her own private counselor, showing up week after week, always asking for her to spill her heart. What was funnier yet was that Leslie felt quite content in doing just that. She didn't feel withdrawn and closed off with Darrin.

"You can't just leave him to find his own way through this," Darrin commented. "I don't think kids are as resilient as we'd like to believe. This is big-time stuff, and he needs real help."

Leslie nodded. "And he's finally getting it. I think once I told my pastor what we were up against, he understood that Travis wasn't getting any better. Now we're getting counseling, but it's like taking five steps back for every one we take forward. Travis hates talking to anyone, but he really hates it when the counselor wants to send me from the room so that he can talk to Travis alone. Travis has developed this real phobia about letting me out of his sight. He has our aunt call down here several times a night, all in order to make sure I haven't been killed."

Darrin frowned. "Do you feel confident about the counselor? I mean, is he qualified to deal with this kind of thing?"

"Oh, definitely," Leslie said, pausing to sip her coffee. "He's a Christian who specializes in dealing with children, and he centers his advice and counseling on the Bible. Of course, he doesn't just sit there and spout Bible verses. After all, Travis is only five."

"I don't think it helps adults to just sit and spout verses, as you say, either." Darrin seemed to search for the right words. "I mean. . .it's just that. . .well, the verses are great, but too often I think people are in the habit of throwing them out like coins. They see someone in need and say, 'Well, here's a verse, now get over your problem and go on with life.'"

Leslie nodded. "Oh, I quite agree. I think there are a great many Christians who have focused on memorizing the words, but not the application behind those words. I've been quoted at many a time, but once in particular I remember asking the woman what she meant by suggesting that particular verse, and she couldn't really explain it."

"I've been there, too. When my mother died from cancer, I can't tell you the number of people that came forward to say, 'Remember Romans 8:28. All things work together for good, to them that love the Lord.'"

Leslie smiled. "I've heard that more times than I care to

remember." She put down her mug. "And, it isn't because I don't believe that, because I do. I believe that God is in everything. I believe that He alone holds the answers to the questions in my heart. But it doesn't make my pain any less to know that He has worked this all out for a purpose and reason. I'm glad God's in the details, but I still hurt, and He knows that."

Darrin looked at her strangely for a moment. "Yet, you find your comfort in Him, don't you?"

She felt a tingling run down her arms. The way he looked at her was so startling, almost as if he could see inside her soul and find the answer for himself. "Yes, I do," she murmured. "And, I find real comfort in His Word. Just as those people who throw out verses without application have sometimes left me frustrated and numb, I've been blessed by a handful of others who have brought genuine direction into my life by sharing Scripture. Just the other day, for example." She paused, looking at Darrin as if to weigh whether or not he really wanted to hear this.

"Go on," he urged without hesitation.

Leslie felt suddenly self-conscious. She glanced around the shop to see if she'd neglected anyone. No one seemed to care that she stood in discussion with one of the customers. Taking a deep breath, she steadied her nerves. "Well, a good friend shared some verses with me from 2 Corinthians 4. I was so moved that I memorized the words, and every day I've used them to strengthen my heart. Not because she threw them out at me and left me to consider them. But because she shared them with me and told me how they applied to her life and how she felt they would apply to my life, as well. Then she prayed with me and even cried with me. It made all the difference in the world."

"And what were the verses?" he asked softly.

Leslie closed her eyes. " 'We are hard pressed on every side, but not crushed; perplexed but not in despair; persecuted but not abandoned; struck down but not destroyed. We always carry around in our body the death of Jesus, so that the life of Jesus may also be revealed in our body. For we who are alive are always being given over to death for Jesus' sake, so that His life may be revealed in our mortal body.'"

Leslie opened her eyes and found Darrin's blue eyes filled with tears. She lowered her gaze and continued. "It meant so much to hear those words and to know that God knew we would have moments of overwhelming heartache and misery, but that we wouldn't be left to bear it alone. That, in fact, it had already been carried to Calvary by His Son Jesus.

"I looked at those verses over and over, and I can still hear the voice of my friend as she shared losing her husband in a plane crash. She told me that she felt so abandoned after his death, but here was proof that she wasn't. She felt completely crushed, crushed in ways that she couldn't begin to explain. Yet here were words that addressed her very feelings, and in that she began to heal, to see that while she was hard-pressed, she wasn't truly crushed. And that while she felt destroyed, in truth she was only struck down for a time.

"She finished up by sharing the very last verses in that chapter, and I'll never forget the love in her voice as she promised me that she knew the truth of those words: 'For our light and momentary troubles are achieving for us an eternal glory that far outweighs them all. So we fix our eyes not on what is seen, but on what is unseen. For what is seen is temporary, but what is unseen is eternal.'"

"That's good advice," Darrin said, pulling out his handkerchief.

He wiped his eyes unashamedly and smiled at Leslie in such a way that she had to swallow her heart to keep it from leaping out of her throat. Who was this man, and why did he affect her the way he did?

The couple at the corner table was getting up to leave, and instantly Leslie felt the spell of the moment broken by their activity. She picked up her cloth from the bleach water and grabbed a tray. "Work calls," she told Darrin as evenly as she could manage.

It wasn't until she was bent over the table and reaching for the couple's empty mugs that she saw how her hands were shaking. A strange feeling washed over her as a thought came unbidden to her mind. Darrin was a remarkable man, and he alone was responsible for these feelings. *But what were these feelings?* Leslie wondered. *Was this what it was like to fall in love?*

She wiped the table and came back to the counter, where Darrin sat with a distant look on his face. *Apparently he isn't moved to ask the same questions of himself,* she thought sadly.

Pushing down her emotions, Leslie nodded to the clock. "I'm afraid it's closing time."

Darrin nodded and put twenty dollars on the counter. "Thanks for the conversation and for the Scripture. I'm going to check it out when I get home." He left her then, and Leslie watched after him until he had disappeared from view.

"You're welcome," she whispered to the empty room and added, "Anytime."

ten

After locking the entrance to Crossroads, Leslie turned the knob and pushed, just to make sure. It was an old habit, but she was sure it had its merits. As she hurriedly walked to her parked car, she felt drawn to look at the stars. It was something she hadn't done for years. Remembering her father, she felt tears sting her eyes. Aaron Heyward was the first person to take the time to introduce Leslie to the sky. He pointed out constellations and planets and was always patient and understanding when her eyes were too untrained to pick out the patterns. Now that she was a grown woman, the sky was no less magical and no less wonderful. And it served as yet another example of how much her parents had given to her.

It wasn't until she had started her car that she realized what time it was. Ten till one. Not too terribly late, but late, nonetheless. She had called Margie around eleven-thirty to tell her that it was a possibility and not to wait up, but no doubt Travis would be waiting. At least nothing had gone wrong tonight. Perhaps that would ease his mind.

Leslie drove carefully down the hill, taking extra care at the Kentucky Street intersection. Within minutes, she was in the driveway of her home. She quickly gathered her purse and gloves and made her way to the door. Upon entering the warmth of the living room, Leslie was surprised to find neither a distraught Travis nor Aunt Margie. Relief washed over her. Maybe they had gone to bed early. This was definitely a good sign.

Wrestling with her coat, scarf, and purse, Leslie found a note taped to the closet door. "We went to bed early—see you

93

in the morning. Margie."

Smiling, she placed her coat in the hall closet and set her boots by the front door. The note said "we went to bed early." That would have to imply that Travis was feeling a little better. At least he wasn't panicked about Leslie getting home. "Thank You, God," she whispered.

For a moment, she just enjoyed the silence of the night. An image of Darrin filtered into her head. She'd really like to know him better. He appeared to be a Christian and enjoy discussions that focused on spiritual matters. He also seemed to genuinely care about the things she told him. Maybe it was just her imagination, but for some reason Leslie got the distinct impression he cared about her. Almost as though she'd known him all her life.

She put such thoughts aside. Her mind was too tired to think about anything more than a hot shower and a soft bed, and there would always be tomorrow to dream about the illustrious Mr. . .Mr. Who? He'd only told her that his name was Darrin.

She pondered the matter only as long as it took to step into the shower. Exhaustion swept over her like the steaming water and lulled her into a state of relaxed disregard. She would let all her worries and troubles wash from her and go down the drain.

Her mother had given her this analogy when she had been a teenager. She could still hear her saying, "Leslie, God tells us to cast all our cares on Him, because He cares for us. When you step into a shower after a hot, dirty game of fast-pitch, you let the dirt and grime wash down the drain without ever desiring to have it back. Just do the same with worry and concern."

"I'm trying, Mama," she whispered, spying the drain with a smile. "I'm trying."

After washing her hair and preparing for bed, she stopped by Travis's room. She could see his still form snuggled under his blankets. The peaceful slumber of his body gave Leslie reason to hope. He didn't thrash about or moan as he usually did during the night. Perhaps tonight there were no nightmares. Perhaps tonight he knew peace. This convinced her not to disturb him. He needed his rest. So did she. Whispering a short prayer for him, Leslie turned and made her way to her own bed.

The next morning, Leslie awoke slowly. The house was totally quiet and peaceful. Closing her eyes tightly, she stretched out her refreshed body under the warmth of her comforter. For a moment, she debated whether or not she should drift back to sleep and enjoy one of the few peaceful times in her hectic life. No, she decided. It would be better to enjoy this time with coffee and conversation. She and Margie seldom had any real time to talk, and Leslie could think of a great many things they needed to discuss. Then, too, maybe Travis would be somewhat recovered, given his early bedtime and uninterrupted slumber. Optimistic thoughts surged through Leslie, urging her out of bed and into her robe.

Leslie hummed as she filled the coffee filter and placed it in the basket of the coffee maker. Maybe she should run down to Joe's Bakery and surprise Margie and Travis with fresh doughnuts. Travis loved it when the glazed doughnuts were warm from the oven and the glaze was still drippy. Her parents had always indulged his love of the sticky pastry, even though cleaning him up was quite a chore. Leslie had always been fond of their baked cinnamon rolls, while her mother had adored the cream puffs. Leslie's father, however, had no favorites. If it was from Joe's, he ate it.

She smiled as she recalled the mornings when her mother would sneak down to the tiny bakery before anyone had awakened. The family would gather in the kitchen and laugh as they ate and drank, enjoying each other's company. How she longed for those mornings again!

Margie padded into the kitchen, still half asleep. She seemed to be guided by the aroma of fresh coffee. "Good morning," she mumbled. "How was work last night?"

"Oh, it went all right. I was glad that I called you, though. I didn't get home until almost one." Leslie handed her aunt a porcelain mug and retrieved one for herself. She filled each with coffee and replaced the pot on the heater. "I was so surprised not to find you or Travis waiting up for me. I hope this means he's getting better."

Margie sipped her coffee and nodded. "It was odd, but he asked if he could go to sleep in my bed for a while. I guess that was around ten-thirty or so. I was exhausted, so the prospect of an early bedtime thrilled me to pieces. He wasn't with me this morning, so I assumed he woke up and went back to his own bed. Isn't he up yet?"

"Nope. I was thinking about going down to Joe's and bringing him some of those fresh glazed doughnuts that he likes so much. I was afraid to just leave without someone being up for him, though. It is odd that he's not around. It's almost eight-fifteen." Leslie poured herself more coffee and sat down at the table with Margie.

"Well, you could check on him, but let him sleep. His body and mind are so exhausted. Maybe this is the best thing for him."

"I'd better get around so I can make it to Joe's before they get cleaned out by the morning rush. I'll check in on Travis first, though. He seemed so peaceful last night that I didn't bother him. Apparently he went back to his bed before I got home," she said, emptying her mug. An unwelcome thought suddenly came to mind. "He didn't seem sick to you last night, did he? I never even thought that he might have a fever or. . ." Her words trailed off as she got to her feet. Motherhood was so new to her that she felt suddenly quite incompetent.

Margie shook her head. "No, he seemed fine. Just very set

on going to bed early. I'm sure he's okay, Les. He's just a very tired little boy."

Leslie relaxed and nodded. "I'm sure you're right. I just don't want to overlook anything."

"You're doing a good job, Leslie. I can't imagine how you could do anything better. Your mom and dad would be proud of you, and so am I."

"Thanks," Leslie said, feeling bittersweet love in the praise. She yawned, stretched, then got to her feet. "I'm going to get dressed."

Upstairs, she selected a pastel blue sweater from her closet and a heavy pair of jeans. Maybe she'd convince Travis to take another walk to the cemetery with her. They'd gone twice before, and both times he seemed to find comfort in the visits. After pulling her hair into a loose ponytail, she put on a pair of thick wool boot socks and went to check on her brother.

Tiptoeing into the small boy's room, Leslie noted that he was still in the same position he'd been in the night before. His body lay completely hidden deep within his covers. Even his head was snuggled under his blankets. She approached the bed and ran a hand along the child's still form and felt goose bumps line her arm.

It didn't feel like Travis. In fact, it didn't feel like anyone. She felt no contour of his body, no arms or legs. Panicked, she turned down the comforter and saw nothing but a pillow. Frantically, she pulled the blankets from the bed, revealing a network of pillows but no Travis.

"Margie!" Leslie screamed. Looking around the room, she noticed several things missing.

The book bag he used on long car trips to fill with toys and picture books.

His favorite teddy bear. It wasn't in his bed or on the floor, like it normally was.

His coat. It was supposed to be hanging on his closet door

knob. It was gone as well. "Margie, come quick!"

Leslie felt the room begin to spin. Where was he? Maybe he was just hiding. Yes, that was it. He was pretending to camp out somewhere in the house like he had done before he had become so withdrawn. Maybe he was in the basement or maybe he was in his parents' bedroom.

"Travis? Travis, answer me! Where are you?" Leslie ran out of the room, nearly flattening Margie against the wall.

"What's wrong, Leslie? What's wrong with Travis?" Margie's face was pale.

"He's gone! I don't know where he is. Oh, Margie. Maybe he's playing that camping game that he and Dad used to play. You know, where he sleeps somewhere in the house and camps out? He's got to be here somewhere. Help me find him!" Leslie tore from room to room, calling his name. "Travis! Travis, honey, please tell Sissy where you are! You're scaring Sissy."

Margie began searching in the opposite direction, but found nothing. Leslie continued yelling and exploring the house. "Travis!" She had checked everywhere. The basement, the bathrooms, the pantry, the closets. Nothing. Travis was nowhere to be found. "Travis, oh, Travis, where are you?"

Suddenly, she felt two hands on her shoulders, gently shaking her. "Leslie, calm down." For the first time, Leslie realized she was sobbing hysterically. What she perceived to be calls to Travis were incoherent screams, reverberating through the empty house. Margie's strong grip guided her back into the kitchen and to the table. "Leslie, stop crying. We need to think."

After being handed another cup of coffee, Leslie quieted herself and concentrated on swallowing the hot liquid. Margie patiently waited for her niece's nerves to come under control.

"Now, what we need to do is call the police, and then the neighbors. Maybe he went over to play with the twins without asking. Maybe he's just testing us. It may not be as bad as we think." Leslie nodded like a frightened child. Margie rose to retrieve the telephone and dialed the police department.

"Yes, I'd like to report a missing child." At this, Leslie began to cry anew, but a sharp look from Margie stifled her sobs.

"My name is Margie Dover. My nephew is missing." Pause. "No, we're not sure how long he's been gone." Again a lengthy pause filled the air with silence. "Five years old," Margie replied into the receiver. "Please, can you send someone over right away?" Margie waited for a moment and then recited the address. "We'll be watching for you. Thank you." She returned the telephone to the cradle and looked over to Leslie.

"They're sending someone over right this minute. It's going to be okay, Les. We'll find him."

"He's just a little boy, Margie. It's so cold outside. I can't believe I didn't check on him. I thought he was asleep, and he hasn't been sleeping well, and I didn't want to risk waking him, so I just went to bed and. . ."

"Les, calm down. Come pray with me, and you'll feel better." Leslie set her empty mug on the oak table and got to her feet. Dejectedly, she walked over to Margie and took her hand. Margie bowed her head, "Dear Lord, our little Travis is out there somewhere, and we know that You are with him, protecting and comforting him. Please help us find Travis, and please keep him safe from all harm. Bring peace to our hearts and guide the police in their search as well as ours. In Your Son's precious name, amen."

Leslie looked up, tears streaming from her eyes. Margie's green eyes also glistened with tears. "It'll be all right, Leslie. God is with us, and He is with Travis. We'll find him." The older woman reached out, and Leslie eagerly accepted the physical contact. Hadn't she just been reflecting on how wonderful the day had seemed?

"Now," Margie said briskly. "It's time to call our neighbors."

Leslie waited anxiously through each phone call. She could tell by Margie's responses that Travis was not to be found. After the last call, the two women simply looked at each other blankly.

A knock at the door brought both women to attention. Margie hurried to usher in the officers, while Leslie tried to still her raging nerves. *If only I'd looked in on him last night. If only I'd. . .*She couldn't help the rampant thoughts that filled her mind.

"So when did you first notice that the boy was missing?" The man's pin identified him as Officer Keats.

Leslie's attention was immediately focused on the man. "I went to check on him after I got dressed," she began. "You see, he hasn't been sleeping well since our parents died. That was about a month ago. Last night, I came home, and he wasn't waiting up for me like usual. I thought it meant he was getting better, so I didn't want to disturb him. This morning, when he still wasn't up, we decided to check on him. That's when I found the pillows."

"And did you notice if anything else was missing?"

"Yes, his favorite teddy bear was gone and his book bag and coat were also gone." Leslie struggled to maintain her calm. "I thought maybe he was hiding because he was angry with me for coming home late or perhaps he was playing a game my father had taught him. It was like camping out, only inside the house. But we searched, and we couldn't find him anywhere."

"Do you have any idea where he may have gone? Neighbors. Friends?"

Leslie and Margie shook their heads. "We've called the only ones we could think of."

"Maybe somewhere he may have felt close to his parents?"

Leslie thought for a moment, and then it dawned on her. "The cemetery. Travis and I walked there often and talked about Mom and Dad. He always talked about wanting to go to be with them in heaven, but I told him that he had to wait until Jesus decided it was time. He liked going to cemetery. It made him feel close to them."

"So you think he might have walked to the cemetery by himself?"

"It's definitely a possibility. It's only about a quarter mile away. I just hate to think of his little body battling the cold. He could have been there all night. There's no telling when he left." Just then, an officer poked his head into the kitchen.

"Hey, I found footprints in the snow leading west. They look child sized."

Leslie nodded. "Yes, the cemetery is west of here. I'm sure that's where he went. We need to get there right now. I want to go along with you." She stood up and retrieved her boots from beside the front door.

"I'll wait here in case he comes back," Margie offered. Officer Keats got to his feet.

"Ms. Heyward, you're welcome to ride with us," he said, striding out of the kitchen and to the front door. Leslie nodded and followed close behind. Forgetting to grab a coat, Leslie shivered violently as soon as she stepped outside. Poor Travis might be out in this. It couldn't be much above zero. Quickly, she got into the squad car.

"You can turn up here at the corner," she said, chattering directions without taking time for a breath.

"I think I know where this cemetery is, Ms. Heyward. Just try to calm down and relax. It'll only take a few minutes before we're there. I'm sure it was a quicker walk than a drive, but just be patient." Leslie nodded. She knew as well as any long-time resident that Lawrence had a myriad of one-way streets, making nearby locations a difficult trip by automobile. That's why it was so much easier to walk than drive.

"Oh, God," she whispered, still shivering from the cold, "please let him hurry. Please let us find Travis, and God, let him be all right."

Moments later, they had arrived at the cemetery. Leslie led them through the headstones to the graves of her parents. She strained to see footprints or anything else that might suggest Travis's approach. *But Travis would have come from the other direction,* she reminded herself. If there were footprints, they wouldn't be found in this area of the cemetery.

Now she was running, and with her she could hear the officers jogging to keep up. Warm air from her lungs streamed from her mouth and nose as she ran. Her lungs ached from the cold and her body protested the abuse, yet she continued, urgently pressing on, needing to know the truth.

They rounded the final corner, and even as they approached, a gasp escaped Leslie's throat. A strangled cry came from her mouth and she stopped without warning, nearly causing one of the officers to plow right into her from behind.

"Oh, God," she moaned unable to find the words to pray. "Oh, please God."

There on the ground in front of her parents' headstone lay the near-frozen body of Travis Heyward.

eleven

Darrin Malone had just finished locking the door of his BMW when he realized the sign at Crossroads read SORRY! WE'RE CLOSED.

"That's odd," he muttered to himself. "I wonder what's going on." Striding up to the entrance, he peered in through the windows, hoping that maybe Leslie had just decided to close early and would be inside counting the drawer or washing off the tables. But much to his dismay, the large room was empty. It was only six o'clock. Where was Leslie or her aunt?

Darrin decided to check the neighboring business. Leslie had said it was run by a man she knew from church. She had mentioned him in several of her conversations with Darrin, and he knew that the family trusted him implicitly. Walking to the door, he struggled to remember. What was his name again? Clayton? No, Blayton? Blanton. That was it. Timothy Blanton. Perhaps he had heard why the store was closed.

Hundreds of worst-case scenarios danced in his mind. Did they have to close the store for lack of customers? Did they get bought out? Was Leslie just tired, and had she decided to take a few days off? Was she too ill to care for Crossroads? His brow furrowed, and his intimidating appearance startled the owner of the nearby shop.

"Excuse me, sir. Are you all right?" A small, bald man hesitantly stepped from behind a counter filled with cookies and chewing gum.

"Well, actually, no. Are you Mr. Timothy Blanton?" The old man nodded slowly.

Darrin sensed the discomfort in the air. He knew his harsh

appearance and blunt questions were, no doubt, unnerving the quiet man's routine. "I came to see if you knew why Crossroads is closed today."

Darrin noticed the man's startled look and offered a weak smile. "Don't worry, I'm not a caffeine addict or anything. I have become a good friend of the owner, Leslie Heyward. She's always there in the evenings. When the store was closed, I automatically assumed the worst. I recalled her mentioning you as a church friend and fellow entrepreneur in a couple of our conversations. That's the reason I stopped by."

Mr. Blanton noticeably relaxed, but just as quickly became somber. "Leslie was unable to be at the store today because of her brother."

"What's wrong with Travis?"

The man seemed nervous and uncertain, but continued. "I don't have all the details, you see. Margie Dover—that's her aunt—called me this morning to tell me that Crossroads would be closed today and possibly for a time longer because Travis was in the hospital. She said something about him running away last night and that they hadn't realized he was missing until this morning. Leslie is spending all her time by his side, and that's why she's unable to run the store. That's all I know."

Mr. Blanton shook his head. "That poor little boy. He just isn't dealing well with the death of his folks. She told you about that, right?" Darrin nodded. "Well, we're praying for the little guy at church, and for his sister and aunt, too. He just doesn't seem to be getting any better."

A few customers entered the small store and immediately headed for the espresso machine near the fountain drinks. "I see her customers are going into withdrawal." Darrin smiled. "Hope she isn't closed for too long. It's a good thing you're here."

Mr. Blanton nodded. "Yep. It may be good for my business,

but I'd give anything to have circumstances be different."

"I understand completely. Thank you for your time. I really appreciate it."

"You her boyfriend?" Mr. Blanton seemed to scrutinize Darrin for a moment.

Darrin laughed, but felt a tinge of. . .well, he wasn't quite sure what it was he felt. "No, I've just come to care quite a bit about her and this situation."

❧

Darrin screeched into the emergency parking area of Lawrence Memorial Hospital. He ran into the hospital and up to the front desk, panting heavily and looking to all the world as though he were a man with his own emergency. As far as he was concerned, this was his emergency.

"Can I help you, sir?" A gray-haired woman smiled sweetly.

"Yes, I hope so. I'm looking for Travis Heyward. He was brought in here earlier this morning. I'd like to go up to the waiting room. I'm just not sure where he is." The older woman's fingers tapped out "HEYWARD, T" on the keyboard in front of her. After a few seconds, a dossier appeared on the screen of the monitor.

"Ah, yes. Here he is. He's in pediatrics." She pulled out a preprinted map and showed Darrin where to go. He thanked her and briskly walked down the long corridor, his mind unable to stop the tumble of thoughts. *What if he's not doing well? How can I help? What should I say or do? Will she understand why I'm here?*

Upon sighting the pediatrics sign, Darrin let out a sigh. He was grateful he hadn't gotten lost. Hospitals were never his forté, even though he had spent so much time in them when his mother was dying. He still managed to lose his way in their maze of sterilized hallways. He wove his way around several visiting people and came upon the waiting room. There, he saw a teary-eyed Leslie. His heart broke in two.

"Leslie?" Her head snapped up.

"Darrin, what are you doing here?" Her face reflected her grief and surprise. She didn't bother to wipe away her tears. How he wished he could see her smile just half as many times as he had seen her troubled and grieving!

"I stopped by Crossroads, but the store was closed. I remembered you saying that Mr. Blanton was a church friend and was familiar with your business, so I asked him if he knew why you weren't there. He didn't know much, except for what your aunt had told him, but he was very helpful. As soon as I heard Travis was in the hospital, my car practically drove itself here." He sat down beside her. "Have you heard anything?"

Leslie shook her head. "Not really. We've been here since around ten. They've come out off and on with bits of information, like his fingers and face are frostbitten. He isn't breathing well—it's real shallow and rapid—but they haven't determined exactly what to do. He's still unconscious," she said, choking back a sob. "The doctors are so busy they don't seem to have time for me. I don't know what to do. I don't know if he's going to. . ." She couldn't finish the sentence.

Darrin reached out to touch her hand. "It'll be all right. You'll see. God will work this out, Les. You have to believe that God is in control of even this." Suddenly, he felt the urge to pray with her, to try and offer her comfort. "Would you mind if we prayed together?"

Leslie brought her bloodshot eyes to meet his. "I'd like that," she said. "I really would."

"Good." He took hold of her trembling hand and bowed his head. "Dear Father, please be with Travis. We don't know all the details, and we're not even sure what's wrong, but we know that You will protect him and keep him from harm. Heal his body, so that it may be as strong as it once was. Give Leslie peace and let her know that Your love is more powerful than

ll the pain and all the trials of this world. And please allow
ne to help them in any way You see fit. In Jesus' name, amen."
He quickly squeezed her hand and felt an odd comfort when
he didn't let go. She needed him there. She wanted him there.
he wanted his help.

"Thank you, Darrin. I am really glad you're here. Margie
topped in for a while, but she seemed so tired and distraught
hat I told her she should go home. I promised to call if I got
ny news, but so far, there hasn't been any, and they're too
usy with him to have me in the room taking up space."

Darrin looked around the empty waiting room. A small
elevision was showing the nightly news. Magazines were
pread generously over end tables and chairs. A soda machine
tood brightly in the corner. The room seemed cold and
onely. Just as he remembered them.

"Can you talk about what happened?"

Leslie nodded and inhaled deeply. "Last night, I came home,
nd he wasn't up waiting for me. Remember I told you that he
lways waits up for me to make sure I really come home?"

Darrin nodded and she continued. "I found a note from
Margie saying they had gone to bed early. That surprised me
o much that I decided not to disturb her or Travis. Especially
nce I saw how still and untroubled his sleep was. At least, I
hought it was him." Her tears began anew.

"This morning, when he still wasn't up at eight-fifteen or so,
ve thought we should check on him, but we didn't want to
vake him if he was finally sleeping well. I went into his room,
nd I folded back the covers to see his face, and all I found
vere pillows. We searched the house and called the police.
When I was talking to them, it came to me that he might have
un away to Mom and Dad's graves. We had walked there a
ew times in the past month, and it wasn't far away. Well, I
vent along with the officers to the cemetery, and there his little
ody was, all frozen and curled up on the ground. It was the

most awful thing I've ever seen. We brought him straight
the hospital. I've been here ever since."

A middle-aged man entered the waiting room, carrying
clipboard. "Ms. Heyward?"

Leslie looked over to the doorway where the man stood
"Yes?"

"I'm Dr. Selig. I'm in charge of caring for your little broth
Travis. I wanted to speak with you about his condition." Dar
noticed her body become rigid. Something about the docto
manner seemed to radiate bad news. "Would you please con
with me?"

Leslie looked at Darrin with sheer terror in her expressio
Without being asked, Darrin got to his feet and put an ar
around Leslie. "Lead the way, Doc," he said, instantly taki
charge.

The doctor led them to a small consultation room, just i
side the double doors that marked the pediatric ward. Darr
helped Leslie to one of the rigid plastic chairs, while the do
tor took his seat behind a small desk.

"I'm afraid, Ms. Heyward, the news isn't good. It seer
that Travis's exposure to the elements has left him quite i
You know about the frostbite to his extremities, but he is al
suffering internally. His lungs were frozen, barely function
when you brought him in. We're doing what we can to war
his body temperature, but he's still critically under normal."

Leslie stared stone-faced at the man, and Darrin put his ar
around her once again.

"What are his chances?" Darrin asked, almost regretting t
words as Leslie turned to look at him in disbelief.

"We aren't confident enough of the situation at this point
really say one way or another. We fear pneumonia will set i
but more troubling at this point is the fact that his body is
fighting as hard as we expected it to. This is sometimes attri
uted to depression, as you informed our nurses that he h

been experiencing. At the moment, he is unstable. I'd like to give you better news, but I just can't lie to you. Your brother is gravely ill and there is a possibility that he may not survive his ordeal. Please know we are doing all that we can."

The last words appeared to be lost on Leslie. She collapsed against Darrin's body. "You can't let him die. He's all I have. You can't let him die."

Darrin held her tight, wishing, praying that he could somehow help her. "Leslie, it'll be all right." He stroked her hair, but it seemed to have no effect.

"I can't deal with this. I can't do this. I can't lose him!" She was gasping for breath.

"Ms. Heyward, you need to calm down. Take deep breaths in through your nose and out through your mouth," Dr. Selig ordered. He called for a nurse, and instantly a petite woman appeared. "Please take Ms. Heyward into the private lounge." Then turning to Darrin he added, "There's a cot there, and I think it would be prudent to have her rest a bit. I know what a shock all of this has been."

"Come on, honey. I'm Kelly. I want you to lie down and rest while I grab you a cold cloth." She helped Leslie to her feet and wrapped a well-muscled arm around her waist. "You aren't going to do yourself any good this way." Leslie didn't even seem to hear her.

They were at the door when Leslie stopped and turned to find Darrin. "Don't go," she barely whispered.

"I promise to stay. I'll be with you in just a minute," Darrin assured her.

Before they could leave the room, a nurse appeared with a stack of papers. "Ms. Heyward, the business office needs to get your insurance information."

"What?" Leslie mumbled, clearly unable to register what the woman needed.

"Health insurance," the woman repeated.

"We don't have any," Leslie replied.

The nurse holding her pushed past the other woman. "M Heyward needs to lie down. I'm taking her to the priva lounge, and you can talk to her there, Amy." The woman no ded and followed.

Darrin realized that without any insurance, Travis's hospit stay was going to be Leslie's total responsibility. With the co of hospitalization, much more so intensive care and eme gency-related services, Leslie could find herself stripped of assets just in order to see her brother received proper care.

"Dr. Selig," he said, turning to catch the doctor before slipped from the room. "I want Travis to have the best poss ble treatment. It doesn't matter what it costs—money isn't problem, and I don't want it to be an issue."

The doctor looked at him indignantly. "I would never wit hold care from a patient because of the financial status of h family."

"I wasn't accusing," Darrin assured, "I'm just stating t facts. That little boy is very important to us."

Selig's expression softened. "I'm sure he is. He's importa to me, as well. Rest assured, I'm doing all that I can. If feel for even one moment that we're compromising his car he'll be airlifted to the University of Kansas Medical Cent in Kansas City."

"Thank you," Darrin said. He hurried out the door, unsu of where they'd taken Leslie. He recognized the woma named Amy and went to speak with her. "Miss?"

"Yes?" The woman looked up from the same stack papers that had accompanied her to the consultation room.

"I want to arrange for Travis Heyward's medical expense As Ms. Heyward said, there is no health insurance, but I wi personally be responsible for the charges." He reached in his wallet and pulled out a business card. "Have all the bil sent here, to my home address."

Amy took the card and jotted down the information. "Are you a relative?" she inquired, handing him back the card.

"No," Darrin replied. "At least not yet." The statement startled him. *Where had that come from?* He had no reason to say such a thing, and yet it seemed very, very right. "Look," he finally said, tearing his thoughts away from the internal questioning, "I don't want Leslie to know about this. I don't want anyone to know that I'm taking responsibility for the bills, understand? Especially not Leslie."

The woman looked at him suspiciously. "No, I don't understand."

Darrin nodded. "It's just that she's a very proud woman. Her business isn't doing well right now, and I know that money is an issue. If you go telling her that I've agreed to take over the payments, she'll reject it in a minute. Just let it go. Let her believe that she'll be billed in the future and that everything is acceptable and under control. That way, maybe once everything is said and done, she'll realize why I did it and accept the help."

Amy smiled. "I get the picture. You must be a very good friend to offer such generous help."

Darrin frowned, thinking of the real reason he and Leslie had come to know one another. "I don't know about that," he murmured. He was suddenly consumed with guilt. None of this would be happening if not for his father's actions. Would there be no end to the sins revisited upon him?

twelve

Only a day had passed since they'd found Travis, but Leslie felt as though it were years instead. She'd refused to leave the hospital and, instead, became a resident of the waiting room along with several other worried parents.

"Ms. Heyward, why don't you go downstairs and get something to eat?" the nurse admonished. It was Kelly, the same woman who had calmed her down after Leslie had heard the truth behind Travis's condition and who had been caring for Travis alongside Dr. Selig. Leslie looked up from her magazine and shook her head.

"No, I'm fine. I'm not hungry. I just don't want to leave in case they find out anything more." Her protests were weak and childlike. But there was no convincing her otherwise. Kelly shrugged and walked back to the nurses' station.

"Leslie, you really should get some rest or eat something. You won't be any good to Travis if they have to put you in the hospital for not taking care of yourself." Darrin put an arm around her, and she didn't resist. She was tired. Very tired. But what if Dr. Selig discovered something new? What good would it do to have her asleep or eating?

"Darrin, I appreciate you being here. Please understand that I don't want to leave here just so I can feel better. There's a little boy in one of those rooms who doesn't have that option, and I am to blame for that." She quieted upon seeing Dr. Selig in the doorway.

"Ms. Heyward? We have some new developments that we thought we should alert you to. You were aware of his frost bite, and due to that, we were attempting to warm his body in

112

the appropriate ways. However, it has recently come to our attention that his body temperature is drastically rising, and he now has a fever of 102 degrees. His breathing has become quite shallow and labored, and now that he has begun to regain consciousness, it's apparent that he is experiencing discomfort in his chest as well."

"What does all this mean?" Leslie interrupted, panicked.

"After listening to Travis's lungs and seeing the X-ray, it has been determined that he is developing pneumonia. We've started him on some very powerful IV antibiotics and put him on oxygen. There's nothing more we can do at the moment. I'm very sorry, Ms. Heyward. If you'd like to see him for a few moments, you might actually catch him awake. Although, I must advise you not to get your hopes up at this point. Even if he is conscious, he won't recognize you or make any sense in the things he might say."

Leslie was immediately to her feet, with Darrin close behind. They hadn't let her see Travis at all, and the waiting was driving her insane. Hurrying to keep up with Dr. Selig, Leslie scarcely paid attention to the brightly decorated children's ward. Travis was in the intensive care unit of pediatrics, and because of this, his room was located just across from the nurses' station.

They stopped outside the sliding glass doors of the room. The clipboard outside read HEYWARD, TRAVIS, along with his date of birth. The doctor perused it momentarily, and before opening the door, he turned to Leslie. "Now, you must understand, it is important that you be prepared for his appearance. Travis is a very sick little boy. The frostbite has left patches of red swollen tissue on his face. The patches resemble burns and may remain in place for several weeks. It just depends on how his recovery goes.

"His lips are swollen and chapped, and because of the pneumonia he has a bit of a grayish-blue tint around them. You need to be as calm and relaxed as possible. If he sees you upset, that, in turn, could upset him, especially given the fact that he's already disoriented from the drugs we're giving him. We just have no way of knowing what he will or won't comprehend, but we have to do what we can to encourage him. Can you handle this?" he asked, great compassion evident in his voice.

Leslie nodded, and Darrin squeezed her hand as the doctor led them inside.

At her first look at Travis, Leslie gasped, but immediately tried to compose herself. It was worse than the doctor had described. Darrin squeezed her hand reassuringly. *Oh, God,* Leslie prayed, *let me be strong for Travis.* She moved to the bedside and watched him stir. His tiny hands and feet were bandaged and elevated. His face was spotted with ugly red blisters on his nose, cheeks, and chin. Kelly checked Travis's monitors and his IV and offered Leslie a tiny smile as she left the room.

Leslie wanted to scoop her brother up and hold him close. Instead she gently took hold of his tiny bandaged hand. *Poor Travis,* she thought. *You shouldn't have to be like this. I should have helped you more. I just didn't know how.*

The small boy stirred and opened his swollen eyes. He mumbled words that were incoherent and barely audible.

"What did you say, baby? Tell Sissy again," she whispered.

"He's been muttering something almost constantly since he began regaining consciousness," Dr. Selig offered. "I'm sure it's just gibberish."

Just then Kelly popped her head back in the room. "Dr. Selig, Dr. Ward wants to speak to you on the telephone."

"I'll be right back," the doctor told Leslie, leaving her and Darrin alone with the beeping monitors and hum of the oxygen unit.

The five year old, barely able to hold his eyes open, again mumbled a series of words.

Leslie leaned down. "Tell Sissy again," she said softly. Travis seemed to struggle for a moment, as if he were fighting the cloudiness that lay between him and full consciousness. He took a breath, and this time the words came clearer. Leslie straightened up as Travis closed his eyes. She felt her heart swell with hope. "Yes, baby, that's right. You remember that," she said, stroking his fine blond hair.

"What did he say?" Darrin asked.

She smiled. "When I'm afraid, I will trust in You."

Darrin smiled. "That's in the Psalms, isn't it?"

"Yes. I told him that verse not long after Mom and Dad died. I told him to use it when he was afraid. I told him that it's what helps me get through scary times."

"Like now?" Darrin questioned. His blue eyes searched her face intensely.

She warmed under his scrutiny. "Yes. This would be the perfect example."

"And do you?" he asked, looking down at Travis, who had closed his eyes again.

She followed Darrin's gaze to her brother's damaged body. "Especially now," she whispered. "How could I ever make it through otherwise?"

❧

The days seemed to drag by, and every day Leslie clung to the hope that this would be the day the doctor would announce Travis's marked improvement. She felt the toll on her body and spirit as one day turned into another and then another, but even more, she saw the price it demanded from her aunt. She felt badly that Margie should have to suffer so much. It seemed that her aunt had aged twenty years in the past week and Leslie longed to offer her comfort, but there was simply nothing left to give.

Leslie was grateful for Darrin's nightly appearances. She still didn't know his last name or where he went during the day, but she knew that every evening at six on the dot, he would appear and sit by her side until it was time to go home. She was coming to count on him more and more, and in some ways it scared her at the same time it comforted her. Why was he being so generous with his time?

She glanced at her watch and smiled. He'd walk through those doors any minute now. A young couple she'd come to recognize entered the waiting room. They were smiling.

"Good news?" Leslie asked hopefully.

"Yes," the mother sighed. "Danny is making wonderful progress. He may even get to go home in another few days. The doctor was particularly worried about his head injury, but the swelling has gone down."

"Thank God," Leslie said, knowing their concern for the eight year old who'd been critically injured in a car accident.

"You can say that again," the father replied. "I never found much need for that kind of mumbo jumbo, but I'm a changed man now. God really proved Himself to me over these last few days."

Leslie nodded and smiled at the sight of Darrin in the doorway behind them. "God has a way of appearing to us in the strangest ways."

"Well, we're going to get something to eat," the woman said, gathering up her things. "See you later."

Leslie waved as they maneuvered past Darrin. "Well, you're right on schedule," she said, finding his handsome face fixed on her.

"You timing me?"

She laughed. "They could hand medication out by your appearance. That's how timely you are. Every night at exactly six o'clock."

Darrin ran a hand through his brown hair. "I can't say that I knew I was exactly that reliable, but I guess I leave the store at the same time every day and it takes exactly fifty-five mintes to fight through traffic and get here."

"Get here from where?" Leslie asked, suddenly feeling relaxed enough to pursue the matter.

"Kansas City," Darrin answered. "I own an antique store called Elysium."

"How fascinating. I would have never pegged you as the type."

"Really? Why not?" Darrin asked, taking the chair beside her.

"I don't know. I guess I saw you more as a lawyer or an accountant or something like that." Leslie shrugged. "Don't ask me why. I guess you just always seemed kind of uptight. Like you had a lot on your mind."

Darrin frowned. His brows knit together in a way that Leslie had come to recognize whenever he contemplated something deeply. "I guess I have had a great deal on my mind of late. Sorry."

"Don't be. I'm the queen of preoccupation, myself." She put down the magazine she'd been trying to concentrate on. "So was it a good day at the shop?"

"Not really," Darrin said, sounding like he'd just as soon forget it. "How about here? Any news?"

"Well, nothing to write home about, but I keep hoping and praying." She stretched her jean-clad legs out in front of her and sighed.

"When did you eat last?" he asked, sounding genuinely concerned.

"Um," she stared up at the ceiling. "I had some coffee this morning."

"Just what I thought. Come on," Darrin said, getting to his feet. "We're going to grab some supper."

Just then Dr. Selig came into the waiting room. Leslie felt her breath catch, and without giving thought to what she was doing, she reached for Darrin's hand and held it tight.

"I have some good news for you, Leslie." She'd finally gotten him to drop the formal sounding Ms. Heyward. "The fever is down, and Travis appears to be responding to the antibiotics."

"Thank God," Leslie said, exhaling the breath she'd been holding.

"So what happens now?" Darrin asked.

"We'll keep up with the antibiotics and continue to monitor him. I'm not counting him out of the woods just yet, but I'd say we've turned a real corner here, and we can look forward to a full recovery."

Dr. Selig left just as quickly as he'd come, but Leslie hardly noticed. She'd thrown herself into Darrin's arms, laughing with joy and thanking God for His goodness. It was only after she'd maintained that position for several minutes that it dawned on her as to what she had done. She could feel his strong arms around her. She could smell the sweet, spicy aftershave he wore. She could hear his heart beating rapidly against the place where she rested her head. Pulling back slowly, Leslie allowed her gaze to meet the questioning expression on Darrin's face.

"Leslie?" Margie questioned from the doorway.

Leslie realized that she still clung to Darrin, and without meaning to appear so startled, she jumped back and swallowed hard. "I. . .we. . ." She laughed nervously, noting the two church friends who accompanied Margie. "The doctor brought good news!" Leslie finally declared. "Travis is showing signs of improvement. His fever is down, and he's definitely responding to the antibiotics."

Margie's face registered instant relief. "Praise the Lord," she said. Turning to her friends, she made the introductions. "Sylvia, Clare, this is Leslie's friend, Darrin." Then smiling at Darrin, Margie added, "Darrin, these are a couple of my dear friends from church. We've been praying together every day for Travis's recovery."

"I'm glad to meet you both," Darrin said, extending his hand. "I'd say the prayers are hitting the mark."

The women smiled, instantly charmed by Darrin's sincerity and broad grin. Leslie watched the exchange, glad that the attention was off her. She felt a strange embarrassment at having her aunt catch her in the arms of a man she hardly knew, yet she couldn't help but remember how good it felt to be held.

"I was just trying to talk Leslie into getting some supper," Darrin said. "Would you ladies care to join us?"

Margie shook her head. "We've just come from Buffalo Bob's, where we ate more than our share. In fact, we've a nice doggy bag down in Clare's car if you two are interested."

"Sounds okay by me," Darrin replied. "You want me to go get it, Leslie?"

"That would be fine," Leslie answered.

Clare gave him the keys to her car, along with explicit directions as to where he could find it. "The front passenger lock is kind of temperamental," she said as he turned to go, "so use the driver's side door."

"Will do," Darrin said, offering a mock salute.

When he'd gone, Margie settled back, a frown drawing lines around her mouth. "I wanted to mention something, but not with Darrin around," she began.

Leslie instantly became aware of her serious mood. "What is it?"

Margie glanced at Clare and Sylvia before continuing. "We've been praying about this, but I don't see any other way than to just come out and say it. We're running out of money, Leslie. There are mortgage payments to be met on the house and rent on the shop, not to mention the utility bills for both places, and the coffee vendor called and said they won't make another delivery unless you pay in full."

Leslie fell back against her chair in defeat. "I have to

admit, the shop has been the last thing on my mind."

"It has to be reopened, and soon," Margie said. "I know you feel the need to stay close to Travis, but. . ."

"But I need to go back to work," Leslie said matter-of-factly. She looked at her aunt and saw the weariness in her expression. Margie hadn't been healthy of late. Worry had sent her blood pressure soaring, and the doctor had put her to complete bed rest at one point. Now, here she was concerning herself over the bills, and suddenly, Leslie felt as though the weight of the world had materialized back on her shoulders.

"Travis is getting better, so it's not like you don't know what's going to happen," Margie offered. "I think I can manage a few hours at the shop in the morning, so you could still come up here and be with him first thing every day."

"No, you know very well what the doctor told you. You can't work," Leslie said sternly. "At least not just yet." She sat thinking for several minutes. "No, I'll go back and just run the shop from twelve to twelve. That shouldn't be too hard on me. It'll only be temporary. If I get home by one, I can get five or six hours of sleep and still spend time with Travis before going to work."

"That won't be easy," Margie said.

"Maybe some of the young people in the church could work at Crossroads," Clare suggested.

"It's a possibility," Margie said thoughtfully.

"I can't afford to pay anyone to work." Leslie's spirit deflated a bit more.

"Here it is," Darrin said, holding up the bag of leftovers like a trophy. "It sure smells good."

"I'll bet it is," Leslie replied, putting on a smile she didn't feel. "Let's eat." She exchanged the briefest of glances with Margie, but it was enough to close the discussion on money and the shop. One way or another, Leslie would figure a way to make it all work. If she didn't, there wouldn't be any hope of keeping the shop, much less of paying Travis's hospital bills.

≈

After Darrin's request to spend a few minutes in private discussion, Leslie finally agreed to leave Margie her car and let Darrin drive her home. She settled into the luxury of the BMW, realizing for the first time just how wealthy Darrin probably was.

"Nice car," she muttered, thinking that the cost of the car alone would probably pay Travis's hospital expenses and the other bills as well.

"What's wrong?" Darrin surprised her by asking.

"What do you mean?" Leslie asked, suddenly feeling quite self-conscious.

"Come on, Les, it's me, Darrin. You were floating on a cloud when I left to get the food, but when I got back you were considerably withdrawn and pretty moody. You want to explain?" He turned into her drive and came to a stop. Shutting off the engine, he turned to face her. "So, what gives?"

Leslie felt her face grow hot. "It's nothing, really."

"Leslie." His voice was soft and patient.

She sighed. "Okay, it's just that I need to reopen Crossroads. The money situation is pretty tight. It's not a big deal, I'll take care of it. I just don't like leaving Travis."

"Why don't you hire some temporaries?" Darrin suggested.

"Who can afford that?" Leslie countered. "We're barely making it as it is, and if I can't recover the loss and pack in some real business between now and the end of the semester, I'll really be hurting by the time summer comes."

"Can I help?" Darrin asked.

Leslie grew suddenly uncomfortable. She undid her seat belt and opened the car door. "I'll be fine, really." She got out of the door and was halfway up the walk when she realized that Darrin was right behind her.

"Leslie, don't shut me out. I didn't mean to embarrass you.

I know this is a tough situation. I just want to help any way I can. You know by now that I care."

That stopped Leslie in her tracks. Turning, she found his expression filled with compassion. Her heart skipped a beat when he placed his hands on her shoulders. She found that words wouldn't come.

"I don't want you to be afraid of how you're going to deal with all of this," Darrin said softly. "I just want you to know that I'm here for you."

"I know that," Leslie whispered. Her voice sounded foreign in her ears. "You've been a good friend, Darrin."

He pulled her into his arms and kissed her long and passionately. Leslie felt goose bumps travel down her spine. His lips were warm and gentle against hers, and for a moment, Leslie forgot who she was and why she was worried in the first place.

"I want to be more than friends," Darrin whispered against her cheek. Leslie began to tremble with the reality of what he'd said. "You're cold," he said, misjudging her reaction. "I shouldn't have kept you out here, but I just had to tell you how I felt."

Leslie forced herself to meet his eyes. Under the glow of her porch light, she could see they were sparked with a fire of passion. "I. . .uh. . .I don't know what to. . .say."

Darrin smiled rather roguishly. "Say that you want to be more than friends, too."

"I. . .I. . .can't," she stammered.

Darrin's expression changed instantly. "Why not?"

"I'm sorry," she said, feeling her whole world spinning out of control. "I just can't go forward with my life until I resolve the past. The accident, my parents' deaths, and now with Travis in the hospital, I just can't."

He smiled again. "Is that all?"

"It's enough," she whispered, feeling tears come to her

eyes. He couldn't possibly understand how badly she'd love to give him the answer he wanted. She needed him. Needed him badly. But Travis had to come first, and the shop needed her now, more than ever.

"Look, I have to go out of town tomorrow. I'll be gone about a week. I'm supposed to fly to Paris and look over some antiques, but I'll be back on Sunday. Can I come see you then?"

"I don't know. I really meant what I said, Darrin. I have a lot of unsorted baggage to go through. A relationship is probably a bad idea right now." She wanted so much for him to understand. She prayed he wouldn't be mad.

"I know what you said," Darrin replied, reaching out to brush back a silky strand of blond hair. "I'll call you Sunday." Then before she could protest, he kissed her lightly on the mouth and left her standing on the walkway.

Leslie couldn't comprehend what was happening. There was too much going on at once, and she felt as though none of it was making much sense. Darrin waved from his car and pulled out of her drive. She found herself waving back, and even though she felt like running after him to bring him back, she stayed rooted in place and marveled at the pleasure she found in his kiss.

"Sunday," she whispered to the cold, winter night. "He's going to call me Sunday."

thirteen

Darrin had barely made it into his apartment when the telephone began its annoying ring. He could tell by the answering machine that it wasn't the first call he'd received that evening. The message line showed the number at ten, and he was certain that most, if not all of the calls, would be from Laurelin.

"Hello?"

"Darrin?" It was Laurelin. "Where in the world have you been? I've been calling all night."

"Yes, I can see that from the answering machine," Darrin said, juggling the telephone and shrugging out of his coat at the same time.

"Well?" Anger edged her voice.

"Well, what?"

"Darrin don't play games with me. You've disappeared every evening for the past week and 'Well, what?' is all you have to say? I want to know what's going on. I've been working myself to death to arrange a caterer for our wedding. The menu is a nightmare, and the prices are outrageous, and you have done nothing to help me! Do you know how many months in advance you need to plan these things? Do you even care?" She barely paused to draw breath. "Oh, Darrin, this is so immature of you."

"Lin, I seriously doubt that maturity is directly proportional to the number of months in advance that one can schedule a caterer. Especially for a wedding that may never take place." He hated himself for just dumping it on her like that. Though she probably deserved to be treated in the manner in which she treated others, Darrin knew it wasn't right for him to be the one to start.

But Laurelin hardly seemed aware of his veiled threat. "Then I've had nothing but problems with Gerda and the shop. You're leaving tomorrow for Paris, and I have to stay here and try to sort through that inventory mess that she created. It just isn't fair."

"Probably not," Darrin said, still amazed that she could ignore his mention of not having the wedding. He sat down, knowing from experience that her tirade could run into the hours if she had her wind up.

"I get the distinct impression that you couldn't care less about my problems."

"Right now, I must admit they are at the bottom of my priority ladder."

"Well, good for you, Darrin," she snapped back snidely. "You go ahead and distance yourself from the conflicts and problems of our world. You've proven to me just what kind of man you are, and what kind of man you aren't. You obviously care very little about anyone but yourself."

Darrin stared up at the ceiling. *If you only knew, Lin,* he thought. Then his conscience was pricked by the fact that she should know. He should just lay it out for her and end their engagement and deal admirably with her. He'd meant to do so weeks ago, but time had gotten away from him, and he'd allowed one excuse after another to keep him from having to deal with her.

"Look, Lin," he finally said, "there's something I need to say here."

"Oh, don't even think of starting in on me. I've had it with your melodramatic, Boy Scout routine. I know you consider yourself one of the last great humanitarians, but I don't buy it. You have a business to run and a fiancée to plan a wedding with. You obviously care very little about either one, but that doesn't change the fact that I care a great deal. I don't want to be the laughingstock of Kansas City when I throw this wedding, and I don't want the business in bankruptcy. I think you'd better give this some definite thought."

"I have given this plenty of thought, Laurelin. That's why I need to say—"

"Don't tell me how much thought you've given this! Your thoughts and time have been consumed by your father's stupidity and that family in Lawrence."

Darrin was shocked that she knew about his dealings with the Heywards. He said nothing, trying to imagine what he could say, but before an answer came to mind, Laurelin was off and running again.

She laughed in a haughty way. "You didn't think I knew, did you? Well, it wasn't that hard to figure out. I thought we'd discussed this, Darrin. I thought I'd made it clear that those people would use you and milk you out of your money. If, and I do mean if, I go through with marrying you, you are going to put a stop to this misguided philanthropic game of yours."

"It's no game, Laurelin," Darrin said, finally moved to the anger Laurelin obviously wanted to provoke. "Those people have a great many problems right now, and I intend to help in any way I can."

"It has to stop, Darrin. You aren't doing them or us any favors. I won't take second place to a group of yokels in Lawrence, Kansas, just because you feel guilty for something you didn't do. Get over it and grow up. I want to marry a man, not a mindless little boy."

"Which brings us back," he said in a very stilted manner, "to the subject of marriage."

"Hardly," Laurelin replied. "I'm not about to continue this discussion with you. Especially not in dealing with the happiest day of my life. You think about what I've said. Think about what you should be doing with your life. After you've come to your senses, give me a call. Then and only then, will we talk about our wedding."

The sound of the receiver being slammed down was no surprise to Darrin. He'd already pulled the phone away from his ear, knowing beyond a doubt what was to follow. For some reason, hanging up first and having the last word gave Laurelin a sense of supreme power and control.

"Well, I hope you sleep better tonight, knowing that I was the last one to hang up," he said into the receiver. He shook his head and hung up the telephone. She probably would sleep better just for having had her chance to berate him. She was like that. A good airing of her soul, and Laurelin was set for another day of living.

He sighed and got up. Staring at the confines of his living room, Darrin was amazed at just how empty it was. There were the normal living room comforts. A sofa, a couple overstuffed chairs, end tables, an entertainment center. He even sported two very fine prints by J. W. Waterhouse on the walls. But it all seemed rather meaningless just now.

Having spent the week with Leslie—having gone through such horrific trauma—he suddenly felt quite lonely not to have her here. He'd known for some time that he was falling in love with her, but there were so many problems to overcome that Darrin didn't dare to allow himself to believe that she might come to feel the same way about him. Hadn't she made it clear tonight that she didn't want a relationship?

"But she definitely responded to my kiss," he said, feeling rather confused by the entire matter.

He paced the room and fought against the urge to call her. *She's asleep by now,* he thought, glancing at the clock to see that it was already midnight. He imagined her face relaxed and peaceful in sleep. She worried so much about everything, and he longed to make it right for her. He wanted nothing more than to protect and keep her, give her the things she needed, support her against the assaults of the world. But she might never accept him, he remembered.

Once she knows who you are, he thought, *she might well hate you for the rest of your life.* But even as that dreaded idea came to mind, Darrin was certain it would never actually happen. *Leslie's not like that. She's not given over to holding someone else accountable for something they didn't do.*

"It still doesn't mean she'd actually want anything to do with me," he said to the air. "Once she finds out that my father was the one responsible for her parents' deaths, she'll probably not hate me, but she certainly won't be able to love me, either."

Frustration and despair began to take root in his heart. He loved her. There was no way he could deny those feelings. He loved her, but he was engaged to Laurelin. "Oh, God," he prayed, suddenly dropping to his knees. "I've made such a mess of things. I need to know what to do. How do I resolve this situation?" The answer seemed evident before the words were even out of his mouth.

Tell them the truth.

Darrin knew it was right. Knew it was the only answer. He had to come clean with both women. He needed to put an end to the deception with Laurelin. He didn't love her. Never really had. He'd found her helpful and savvy, but those were certainly not reasons to marry. No, he had to tell her the truth and do it very quickly. Then a thought came to him. He was leaving in the morning for Paris. There would be no chance to tell her anything until he got back.

"Okay, God," he prayed. "I know this is all my fault. I've tried to make up for my father's sins, and I've tried to take responsibility for things that had nothing to do with me. I spent a lifetime distancing myself from my father, yet now I openly accept the problems he created, and the results are eating me alive. Show me what to do, and when. Direct my steps, and show me beyond a shadow of a doubt how to deal with each problem as it develops so that I don't find myself in this mess again."

Darrin instantly thought of that night in Dallas when he'd first learned the truth about the Heywards and his father. He thought back to the Scripture God had clearly given him for comfort and inspiration. Getting up, he went to his bedroom and took up his Bible. Sitting on the edge of the bed, he thumbed through until he came to the verse in Ephesians 4: "Let all bitterness, and wrath, and anger, and clamor, and evil speaking, be put away from you, with all malice: And be ye kind one to another, tenderhearted, forgiving one another, even as God for Christ's sake hath forgiven you."

Darrin sat staring down at the page for a long time. "For Christ's sake," Darrin murmured. "God forgave for Jesus' sake, and I have to forgive for the same reasons. Not because I'm some great guy who can just overlook the bad things in my life or the wrongs people have done. But because Jesus died and paid a very real price for those things. And because I am to be like God, forgiving and giving of kindness and love."

Peace began to filter into Darrin's heart and soul. There were many things that needed to be released from his hold. He needed to forgive his father and let go of the past mistakes and injuries done to him by the man. He needed to forgive Laurelin and to ask her to forgive him as well. He'd wronged her by agreeing to marry her for all the wrong reasons. He needed to seek Leslie's forgiveness, too. Not for what his father had done, but for not telling her right up front who he was and why he initially cared.

"Help me, Father," he whispered. "Help me to set things right. Help me to pick up the pieces and put them back where they belong."

fourteen

Leslie found herself excited at the prospect of Darrin's return to the States. He'd told her he would call on Sunday and that would be tomorrow. She couldn't help but replay the scene between them when he'd kissed her. A real fire had ignited in her heart that night, and it was hard to ignore the effects it had on her. Just as the Kansas weather had changed and spring had finally shown signs of arrival, love had begun to bloom in her frozen heart. She still suffered from the conflicting emotions, remembering what he'd said to her and what she'd said in reply. She'd put him off, but he hadn't really been persuaded by her meager attempt.

"But it was the truth," she said aloud, as she moved around the small storage room at the back of the shop.

Taking down several bags of gourmet blend coffee, she sighed. "He wants to be more than friends." She smiled. She couldn't help it. How long had she prayed that a Christian man would come into her life and speak just those words?

With less than twenty minutes until time to open the shop, Leslie suddenly remembered that she needed to call the hospital. Travis was due to come home in a few days, and she still had no idea what the cost of his care had mounted to over the last two weeks.

Stacking the coffee behind the counter, she went to the telephone and dialed the main number for the hospital. "Business office, please," she told the operator and waited patiently while the call was connected.

"Business office," a pleasant-sounding woman answered.

"Yes, this is Leslie Heyward. My brother Travis is a patient there at the hospital, and I wanted to check on the status of his bill. I just want to get an idea of what the total is at

130

this point."

"Well, that will be rather difficult to say, especially since he's still a patient. Charges come in every day, you understand, and there won't be an account total at this point."

"Yes, I understand all that. I just wondered if you could give me an idea of what it has come to so far. You see, we don't have insurance, and I need to be checking into ways to collect the money. If I don't have some kind of idea, I'll be trying to do everything at the last minute."

"Of course, I understand. Let me see," the woman paused, and Leslie could hear the clicking of computer keys. "You said the last name was Haywood?"

"No, that should be Heyward," Leslie replied and spelled the name slowly. "Travis is the first name."

"Oh, yes, here it is. Hmmm, he spent time in intensive care, right?"

"Yes, that's right. He's in a regular room now, however."

"Well, just in keeping with what we have so far, which is current to a point of the charges submitted, I'm showing a total of $12,211."

"What?" Leslie said, stunned by the vast numbers being thrown at her.

"A little over twelve thousand dollars," the woman replied. "Of course, that doesn't include the doctor's charges. He'll bill you separately for his work."

"I had no idea," Leslie said, taking the phone over to a counter chair where she could sit down. She felt as though the wind had been knocked from her. "And you say the charges are still coming in?"

"Well, yes. After all, he's still a patient. The charges will continue to come in for several days after he's dismissed. You know how it is—several departments with a variety of tasks performed. They try to submit their charges quickly, but it takes time. You will be given a printout of all charges on the date of dismissal, but a complete listing might take as much as thirty days to compile. We'll mail you one when it's complete."

"I see," Leslie said, still unable to fathom where she was going to come up with the money. "Do you have any estimate of what I might expect if he stays another, say three or four days?"

"Well, of course, it depends on what he needs during those days, but I would just round it off to fifteen thousand. Especially given the fact that you have no idea what Dr. Selig's charges will be. I see his name listed on the chart here, but if you had any other doctors assisting him, you'll want to remember they will be mailing you charges as well."

It was more than Leslie could deal with. "Thank you for your help," she said rather curtly and got up to hang up the phone. "What am I going to do?"

She looked around her at the shop and felt despair like she'd never known before. "Fifteen thousand dollars? Oh, God, where am I going to get that kind of money? Please, God, show me what to do."

She thought of her accountant, Bill Pendleton. He was a good friend and a Christian whom she'd met at church long ago. She quickly dialed his number, and when his wife answered the phone, Leslie apologized for disrupting their Saturday and asked to speak with Bill.

"Bill, it's Leslie Heyward. I have something I need to ask you. It's pretty overwhelming and I didn't know what else to do."

"That's quite all right, Leslie. That's what I'm here for."

"Bill, I just talked to the hospital business office about Travis's expenses."

"Say, how's he doing? I heard from my mom that he might be coming home soon."

"Yes, we're hopeful of that. Maybe another three or four days if he continues to progress the way he has been."

"That's great news. So what happened with the billing

office?" In the background a loud crash of some sort disrupted the peaceful conversation. "Leslie, just a minute," Bill said into the receiver. She heard him instruct his children to go into the other room, and within seconds he was back on the line. "Sorry about that. You were saying?"

"Bill, the hospital says that I can expect Travis's account to total fifteen thousand dollars, and that doesn't include Dr. Selig's services."

Bill whistled. "Wow, that's quite a chunk."

"Yes, and we have no insurance." There was dead silence on the other end of the line. "Bill, I don't know what to do about this. Will they let us make payments at the hospital? Can I take a loan for that kind of money? Should I get a second mortgage on the house?"

"Oh, boy," Bill said, obviously overwhelmed with the news. "That's a good question. Well, right off the bat I can tell you that the hospital isn't going to want to carry a fifteen-thousand-dollar balance, but I'm not sure what their rules are on such things. As for a second mortgage—it's out of the question. The bank isn't going to be too inclined to give out money, even though you have good equity in the house. Your only source of income is the shop, and from the last statement you sent me, business is way off. On top of that, you're already behind in the rent, so I doubt the bank would be willing to offer you much. Certainly not fifteen thousand." He fell silent for a moment, then added, "Look, I'll do some checking into this and get back to you."

Leslie sighed. "I guess that's all I can ask of you."

"Don't let this get to you, Leslie. Take it to God in prayer, and I'll do likewise. There has to be an answer, and God hasn't let you down yet."

"I suppose you're right," she murmured.

"Let me call around, Leslie, and don't go trying to do anything on your own, okay?"

"You mean like put the shop equipment up for sale?" she

said, only half joking.

"Exactly," he replied quite seriously. "If it comes to that, I'll help you make the necessary arrangements, but Leslie," he paused and his voice softened, "it doesn't necessarily have to come to that."

"Okay, Bill. If you say so." She knew the despair was evident in her tone.

"One last thing, Leslie."

"Yes?"

"Would it bother you if I shared this information with some of the other businessmen in the church? I mean, two or three or even more heads may well be better than one in this case."

"No, I don't have a problem. Everyone there knows the circumstances well enough," Leslie replied. She knew, too, that the people of her church genuinely cared about her. "Go ahead and do what you need to, and I promise to wait until I hear from you."

"Good girl."

She hung up the telephone without having gained any sense of peace or comfort from the call. Even her accountant didn't know what to do, and that wasn't a very encouraging thought.

"Dear God," she prayed. "There has got to be a way through this. I believe that, and I know with Your help, nothing is impossible. It just really feels that way. I need You to give me strength and to give me peace. Please let me rejoice in Travis's health, and don't let the financial aspects of his recovery draw my attention away from the gift You have given me. Thank You for all You have done and continue to do. Amen."

For a moment, Leslie stood perfectly still, allowing God's peace to fill her heart. It would all work out. She knew it would, because God was with her. With that knowledge, she went back to preparing Crossroads for opening.

"Leslie? This is Bill." Disappointment flooded Leslie's heart. She had hoped the ringing phone would bring Darrin's voice into her house.

"Hi, Bill. Sorry I didn't talk to you at church this morning, but Margie wasn't feeling well and I wanted to get up to the hospital to see how Travis was faring."

"I understand," he said, not sounding at all comfortable with the conversation.

"What is it, Bill? Did you find out something I should know about this financial mess?"

"I talked to some of the guys at church. In fact, we chatted about half an hour together after the service. I'm afraid we didn't come up with any concrete solutions. In looking through all of your financial information, the options are quite limited. I've asked around, and unfortunately, it does seem you may well end up having to sell Crossroads. I mean you don't want to wait until it's gone under, and you can't recoup anything from the sale. I am really sorry. I didn't believe it would have to come to this, but. . ."

"I understand, Bill." Leslie felt the bottom drop out of her world. "Thank you for your help. You will come over to help me put things together—you know, decipher the paperwork and such?" Leslie's stoic voice masked the turmoil of emotions within her.

"Of course, I will, honey. Don't you worry. I want you to know that we're all here for you. I think you've done an outstanding job taking care of everything. Your mom and dad would really be proud." Leslie could almost see his face, filled with compassion and fatherly love. Bill had always been such a good friend. She knew the prospect of selling Crossroads was just as upsetting to the Pendletons as it was to her and Margie. She had grown up knowing the Pendletons as a second family, and Leslie appreciated their unconditional support.

"Thanks, Bill. Keep me posted, all right?"

"Definitely. Bye, Les."

"Good-bye, Bill." Leslie hung the telephone back on the cradle.

Leslie changed out of her Sunday clothes and pulled on jeans. All the while she kept hearing Bill's voice in her head. *Why, God?* she asked, taking out a long-sleeved white oxford blouse. *Why?*

Doing up the buttons, Leslie felt despair take deep root in her heart. Crossroads had been such an important part of her life. How could she give it up now? How could she sell a business that her parents had created and run profitably all those years, all in order to pay an outrageous hospital bill?

But it's not outrageous, she thought. The hospital and doctors had given her back Travis. Oh, she knew full well that it had come at God's hand, but they were the instruments God had chosen to use. How could she fault them for charging for their services? She would gladly pay ten times the amount they charged, if it meant Travis would live.

The rattle and crash of pans in the kitchen brought Leslie back to reality.

Margie. Leslie hadn't said much to Margie about the hospital bill nor the situation regarding how it might be paid. She'd wanted to save the older woman any upset if it turned out that their worries had been for naught. Now, however, it appeared she was going to have to give Margie the nitty-gritty details and pray it didn't cause her blood pressure to soar out of control.

"Margie," Leslie called, coming into the kitchen. Her aunt was already changed and working on Sunday lunch.

Turning to face her niece, Margie frowned. "Is something wrong, Les? Was that the hospital calling?"

"No, it wasn't the hospital, but well, actually something is wrong. That was Bill Pendleton. I had called him yesterday after talking to the hospital about Travis's bill."

Margie's face paled a bit. "How bad is it?"

Leslie tried not to appear overly concerned. "Around fifteen thousand." She held up her hand before Margie could say anything. "That's not the exact total so it could be less."

"Oh, dear."

Leslie worried that Margie herself would soon be in the hospital if she didn't sit down and relax. "Here," Leslie said, pulling out a kitchen chair. "Sit down, and I'll tell you as much as I can."

Margie did as instructed, casting a worried gaze upon Leslie. "Don't lie to me about any of it, Leslie."

"I didn't plan to," she replied. "I worry about upsetting you, so please understand that no matter what I tell you, I believe God will see us through this."

"All right," Margie replied. "I agree with that philosophy, so lay it on me."

Leslie took a deep breath. "Bill thinks we're going to have to sell Crossroads."

"Oh, no!"

"I didn't want to worry you until I knew for sure. The only way I could see to deal with it was to sell the store, but Bill wanted to talk to some other men from the church before we decided. I guess they arrived at the same conclusion. If we wait too long, the store will lose even more value and the debts against it will climb. So we need to move right away on it."

"Leslie, this is awful. What are we going to do?"

"All that we can do, Margie. Leave it in God's hands. We always said the store was a service to Him. Even the name Crossroads was given with an intention of ministry behind it. Maybe we've done our work and it's time to move on."

Leslie paused to look heavenward. "Maybe it's even time to sell the house and get something smaller. Travis and I don't need much room, and you still have your apartment. If I work a normal job with regular hours, maybe I can be there for Travis in a better way, and he can get over the emotional damage he's suffered. I just don't know, but what I do know is that I have to step forward in faith. I have to keep going."

"Yes, yes. I know. I just hate to think of you doing this alone."

"I'm not alone. I have God. Everything will work out fine. You'll see. With or without Crossroads, as long as Travis is well and we have each other, we will be fine."

◈

After lunch, Leslie drove the familiar route to the hospital. She was excited to see Travis, knowing that each day he seemed to be growing stronger and more healthy. As she made her way through the pediatric wing, she smiled and waved at the different nurses and doctors whom she had come to know as friends. Kelly looked up and nodded a hurried greeting as she filled out some paperwork for the doctor looming over her shoulder. Amy came over and chatted on the way to Travis's room.

"Oh, he's doing *so* much better, Leslie. All the doctors are really impressed with his recovery. What a little trooper he is!" Amy's brunette ponytail bounced with each step she took. With all that energy and optimism, it was no wonder she was assigned to work with recovering children.

"Yes, I am so grateful for all that has been done to help him. You guys really are a Godsend." Leslie smiled broadly as soon as they entered Travis's room. "Ah, there he is! How's my favorite five-year-old?"

She was relieved to see that the blisters on his face were healing, though Dr. Selig assured her the skin would be tender for months to come. His hands were unbandaged, and the pink skin against his pale arms made him look like he was wearing gloves. Despite her brother's injuries, Leslie still believed him to be the most handsome boy in the world.

"Hi, Sissy," he said brightly.

After checking his IV and his various monitors, Amy nodded satisfactorily. "Well, I guess I'll leave you two alone. You seem very healthy, Mr. Heyward." The little boy beamed at the compliment, and after ruffling his blond hair, Amy left Leslie and Travis in silence.

"So, how are you feeling, honey?" Leslie pulled one of the chairs next to his bedside and gingerly held his rosy hand.

"I feel okay, Sissy." His face assumed a somber look. "I miss my toys, though."

Smiling, Leslie nodded sympathetically. "I'll bet you do. There doesn't seem to be much fun stuff for a little boy to do in here."

"Nope," Travis shook his head sternly. "And I need fun stuff. I'm a fun boy."

"You sure are, Travis. You are definitely a fun boy. But you'll be back in your fun room soon."

Travis's eyes brightened. "Really? I'll be home soon? How many days?"

"Well, Dr. Selig says that you should be able to come home in a couple days. Unless something else happens."

"Nothing else is going to happen. I'm all better."

"I know, honey. But the doctors want to make sure. You don't want to have to come back here after I get you home, right?" Travis shook his head. "Well, then, you need to listen to Dr. Selig and do everything he says. Pretty soon, I'll be able to take you home."

For a moment, Travis was quiet. His tiny brow was furrowed, and his eyes were focused on the ceiling. "Leslie, I wanna talk to you."

"Sure, baby. What about?"

" 'Bout God. And heaven. And Mama and Daddy."

"Okay. What did you want to say?"

"Well, I been thinking 'bout what you said 'bout how when Jesus wanted me to come home to heaven, He'd tell me so. And when I went out to see Mama and Daddy that night, I thought I heard Jesus."

"What did He say to you, honey?" Leslie softly stroked his arm as he tried to put words to his thoughts.

"I thought He said I could go home," Travis replied.

"Maybe He was telling you to come back home before you got sick," Leslie offered with a smile.

"I really wanted to go to heaven, Leslie." His five-year-old face appeared very serious.

"I know, sweetie. It's okay to miss Mom and Dad, but you have to understand that they are gone and waiting for us in heaven. We can't just pick up the phone and call for God to come get us and take us to heaven, too. We can pray, though. We can tell God how much it hurts, because you know what, Trav? He already knows our pain. He knows how much you hurt and how much you miss your mama and daddy."

Travis seemed to grow distant for a moment, so Leslie got up and carefully lifted him in her arms before settling into the bed herself. She lay there with him snuggled in her arms. "Don't go away, Travis," she said, her eyes growing moist. "Don't go away and leave me. I need you. I love you."

Travis hugged her tightly. "I love you, Sissy. I won't go away again."

Leslie sniffed back her tears. "I know this is hard for you to understand, but I don't want you to go away in your mind, either. I want you to talk to me when you're upset or scared. I want you to trust me to be there for you when you need me. Travis, I know I'll never be as good a parent to you as Mom and Dad, but I will take care of you. I won't let anything bad happen to you, if you'll just let me help you."

"I don't know what you mean," Travis said, pushing away from Leslie enough to look into her tear-filled eyes.

"I mean that I don't want you to hide from me or from God." Leslie reached up with one hand to touch his head. "I don't want you to hide away inside your mind. Do you understand? I don't want you to stop talking to me. I don't want you to think that you can't tell me what's going on in here." She tapped his head gently.

Travis looked at her strangely, and Leslie knew she wasn't getting through to him. "What I mean, Trav, is that when you think about Mom and Dad, it's okay to talk to me about it. If you want to remember a funny thing and laugh about it, that's okay. If you want to talk about the accident and how bad it feels that they died, then I want you to know that I will be happy to talk to you about that as well. I just want you to know that you can talk to me about anything. Even if you think that I'll think it's silly. You are important to me.

"If you're afraid of cars, then I want you to say so, and together we'll figure out a way to help you through it. If you can't sleep at night because you have bad dreams, then come to me, and I'll sit with you, and we'll pray together until you feel better. Do you understand now, Travis?"

"I think so," he said, falling back against her. "I can talk to you like I did Mommy."

Leslie felt a lump in her throat, remembering all the times she had turned to her mother in fear or despair. "Yes," she answered softly. "I'll never be able to take Mommy's place, but I don't want to take that place, either. I want to be your big sister, and I want to be your friend."

Travis nodded. "And I'll be the brother."

Leslie laughed softly and patted his back. "Yes. You will be the brother and the fun boy, and the joy in my otherwise dismal world." She hugged him tightly, feeling the blessing God had given her in Travis. Healing had truly begun for both of their spirits. Together, they stood in the middle of a crossroad, and together they had chosen a path of healing. *If only Darrin could be here,* Leslie thought, and the idea of sharing this small step forward seemed of major importance to her. Suddenly a great idea came to mind. She wouldn't wait for him to call her. She would call him. He'd given her his phone number when Travis had first been admitted to the hospital.

"Hey, Travis," she said with absolute joy filling her heart. "How about we call Darrin?"

fifteen

Even with the effects of jet lag lingering in his system, Darrin had decided to speak to Laurelin at the first possible opportunity. All the time he spent in Paris, he kept thinking about how on Sunday he would go to Lawrence and spend the day with Leslie. But in the back of his mind, the nagging reminder that he had to deal with Laurelin wouldn't allow him so much as a phone call to Leslie. Now Laurelin was due at the apartment any minute, and Darrin was nervously filling his time making iced tea.

He'd prayed a great deal about what he intended to tell her. He wanted to witness to her, but knew it wouldn't be well received, especially in light of the fact that he intended to break their engagement. Laurelin would expect him to have gotten his act together and be prepared to go forward with the wedding.

A knock at the door announced her arrival, and Darrin breathed a prayer before allowing her admittance.

"Hello, Lin."

Laurelin breezed into the house, wearing a complimentary spring suit of pale pink linen. "Well, hello yourself," she said with a sunny smile. "The weather outside is absolutely perfect. It's a gorgeous afternoon. Have you been outside?"

Darrin shook his head. "No, but I could see that things were showing definite signs of spring."

"So how was Paris?"

Darrin smiled. "Cold, rainy, and tiresome."

"Tiresome? Never!" Laurelin declared good-naturedly.

Darrin was surprised by her pleasant mood, yet he proceeded forward with extreme caution. He knew just how volatile this woman and her moods could be. "So," he said in a casual fashion, "would you care for some iced tea? I just

142

ewed a pot and was getting ready to pour it over ice."

"Sounds great. Don't forget the lemon." She sauntered over
the sofa and made herself at home. "Well, in spite of the fact
at you found Paris a drudge, I'd say it did wonders for you.
ou don't seem nearly as uptight as you were before you left."

Just then the telephone rang, and Laurelin reached over.
'll get it."

Darrin said nothing, seeing absolutely no reason why it
ould hurt anything for her to answer the phone while he
as busy with the tea. He could hear her speaking, but couldn't
ake out the words. Whoever it was, she seemed quite capa-
e of handling the situation.

She was just hanging up when Darrin returned with two
asses in hand. "Who was on the phone?" he asked.

"Wrong number," Laurelin purred, taking the offered tea.
So we were talking about you and how you aren't nearly as
sty as you were before you left."

Darrin nodded and took a seat in one of the overstuffed
airs. Laurelin frowned at him for his obvious distancing,
t she said nothing.

"A lot of answers have come to me while I was gone. I
ppose that's why I don't feel so 'testy' as you put it. There
as plenty to do in Paris, but I spent most of my downtime,
e time I could have to myself, in prayer."

Laurelin rolled her eyes. "We aren't going to talk about that
gain, are we?"

"I'm afraid so," Darrin said apologetically. "Because it has
verything to do with what I need to say, to you."

Her hand stopped with the glass of tea midway to her lips.
What are you trying to say, Darrin?"

"I'm trying to tell you that I can't marry you, Lin. I don't
ve you anymore. I'm not sure I ever loved you the way I
ould have, but I know for sure that I can't marry you feeling
e way I do."

"Well, isn't that nice," Laurelin said rather snidely. "It's someone else, isn't it? That's where you've been spending all your time, isn't it? Of all the selfish, self-centered people, you really take the cake, Darrin Malone. I've spent a great deal of time and effort putting together this wedding, and now you sit there ever so calmly telling me that you can't marry me because your *feelings* have changed. Well, I'm not going to let you do this to me. Do you have any idea how much time has gone into this? The effort on my part has been immeasurable. I've had to do this on my own, and now you tell me it was for nothing. Darrin, you don't deserve me." Her brown eyes sparked.

"No, Lin, I suppose I don't. But then again, I'm not sure who does." He watched as a smile played at her lips. She had taken it as a compliment. Hadn't he known that she would. Darrin attempted to remain calm. After all, he knew in his heart he was doing the right thing. He had expected no less from Laurelin. He couldn't blame her for being angry. But her vicious rantings always hit a nerve in him, and he wasn't sure how long he could maintain his composure.

"Laurelin, this was not a snap decision. For a long time things have not been right between us. I have taken this to God in prayer, and I feel led to tell you the truth. The truth is, I can not and I will not marry you. I felt like I had to keep on with the relationship because of how convenient you were. . .with the store, with my trips, with my life. That was not fair to you and I apologize. I tried to convince myself we really were alike, when in reality, we were complete opposites, in spirit, if nothing else. You don't believe like I do, and you don't want to. I refuse to be unequally yoked with you." Darrin took a long sip from his iced tea and awaited her reply.

"So you're leaving me because of a God thing? Darrin, that's no reason to end a relationship. People get married all the time without believing the same way. There's got to be something more. You don't really believe this religion excuse and neither do I."

She leaned forward in a menacing manner. "So, who is

Darrin? Someone you met in Paris? Another antiques dealer? Someone who shows more promise than I do? Tell me."

Darrin rolled his eyes. "Yes, it is a 'God thing' as you so eloquently put it. I'm sorry if you don't believe my 'excuse,' but it's the truth. I don't feel I have anything in common with you except the shop, and that's not enough to base a marriage on. I am not going to continue in a relationship where I provide no more than critical insight to your wardrobe choices and decorating techniques.

"I need to feel I can confide in you, take my fears to you, and that you will meet me halfway with love and compassion. I don't feel you are prepared to do that. As a matter of fact, I don't think you ever will be. You love Laurelin Firth and her interior decorating business. You don't love me, you don't love our relationship, and you definitely don't love God. Now, how do you propose a marriage under such conditions?"

"If you wanted it bad enough, you'd make it work. You are a quitter, Darrin Malone. You have no drive, no desire. You cut your losses and run if things don't go your way. So I didn't turn out the way you thought I would. You certainly didn't seem to mind a year ago, or even six months ago. Now you're telling me you've had this epiphany, and you realize that you can't marry me because I don't believe like you. I don't buy it! You'll be a loser without me, Darrin. You remember that. If you leave me, Elysium will fall in ruins. You think Gerda will pick up my slack? And just what am I supposed to do without that job?"

"Lin, if you want it, the job is still yours. I don't expect you to rely solely on your interior decorating." Darrin stretched out his long legs and took another drink of iced tea. This wasn't going well at all. He could tell that nothing he said made any difference to her. She had just been dumped. And that didn't happen to Laurelin Firth. Her veiled threats and snide comments were meant to keep Darrin on his toes, not push him over the edge. Now, she didn't know how to react.

"You know, Lin, it occurred to me that this is the one scenario you probably haven't rehearsed. That's what bothers you so much, isn't it? I've put you into a very uncomfortable situation, and you don't know how to deal with it any other way than to be nasty and hurtful." He watched as Laurelin's face dropped in horror.

"How dare you imply that I don't know how to deal with you? You're nothing, Darrin. Nothing at all. I'm not being nasty—I'm being realistic. Something you obviously haven't taken the time to be. I know exactly how to deal with you and your childish desires. You felt smothered and trapped, like all men do when facing a marriage, and you panicked. Then, to save yourself from looking like a noncommittal little boy, you whipped up this 'believer/nonbeliever' jazz because you knew that if all else failed, you could throw Bible verses at me and look all superior. 'See? I really can't marry you. Look how many verses I know that you don't.' That's all it is. And yes, I'm angry, and I have good reason to be. But don't you ever tell me that I don't know how to deal with something. I always know how to deal with everything."

Darrin couldn't recall a time when he'd seen her so upset. She was breathing heavily from shouting for almost five minutes without a rest. Her fists were clenched, and her teeth were gritted.

"Lin, think of it as you like. No doubt that's the version our friends will receive. I really don't care. You can't touch me with your words. What I have told you is the truth. My faith is growing stronger, and I am seeing you in a different light. I don't love you anymore, and whether or not I ever did is in question, as well. It's over. No amount of screaming is going to change that. And as to whether or not there's someone else, yes, there may very well be. But that is none of your business."

Laurelin grabbed her purse and abruptly stood up. "Fine, Darrin. Have it your way. It's over. Great. And I suppose I'm the one who gets to break it to everyone. Well, thanks a lot. At least I'll have more time on my hands." Dejectedly, she ook her head. "All those wedding napkins. Wasted. What in e world am I going to do with all those napkins?"

"Look, Laurelin, I don't want this to end badly. I really feel rrible about this, because it is my fault. Will you ever be able forgive me?" He genuinely meant it. He didn't relish the ought of a slighted Ms. Firth being in charge of his antiques hile he was away, and he truly didn't want her to be hurt and gry. She couldn't help who she was, nor could he.

"It's going to take a lot of effort on my part, Darrin, but I will y. I'm not promising anything, you know." Darrin nodded.

"No, of course you're not. How could you?"

"Another thing," she said angrily, "you can keep your job d your stupid store. I'll be fine without any handouts from ou."

He watched as she confidently strode to the door of his partment. Just before walking out, she turned. "Oh, and one ore thing. You might want to call Leslie."

Quickly, she slammed the door behind her, leaving Darrin's oughts in turmoil. Leslie? How did she know about Leslie?

Suddenly, he understood. It hadn't been a wrong number hen he was in the kitchen. Laurelin had spoken to Leslie. No oubt, Lin's sarcastic and superior nature had left Leslie bat-red. She probably hated him now.

What if she was calling about Travis? What if he was worse? *h, Lord,* he prayed. *Please let Travis be okay. And please on't let Leslie be angry.* Dialing the number to her home, arrin's frustration grew. The busy signal offered him little omfort.

"Come on, Leslie, get off the telephone."

He tried for over an hour, and still the same pulsating drone ame back in his ear. His worry and concern for Travis began eat at him, so rejecting Leslie's home phone, he dialed the ospital instead.

The hospital operator sounded less than cheery, but Darrin eld back any comment and asked instead to speak to the nurses' desk in pediatrics.

"Pediatrics, this is Kelly," came the voice.

"Kelly, this is Darrin Malone. Travis and Leslie Heyward' friend, remember?"

"Oh, sure. What can I do for you?"

"Well, I've had to be out of town for the past week, and wondered how Travis was doing. I'd tried to call Leslie, bu her line is busy."

"Oh, well, you just missed her. She was here up until abou five minutes ago. Travis is great. He may get to go home in couple days."

Darrin breathed a sigh of relief. "That is good news."

"Darrin, I'm real sorry, but I can't hang on. I've got twe new patients coming in and—"

"That's okay, Kelly," Darrin interrupted her explanation. " just wanted to make sure Travis was okay."

"Sure thing."

For several seconds after Kelly had hung up, Darrin jus stood in place, phone in hand. Why had Leslie called if Travi was recovering so well? Was something else wrong? Or. . .He smiled to himself. Maybe she'd changed her mind about bein more than friends.

He replaced the receiver and picked up his iced tea. The urg to go to Lawrence battled with the fatigue he felt from the lon flight. *Maybe I'll just grab a nap and then go over,* he though with a yawn. That sounded exactly perfect. He'd just take quick nap and drive to Lawrence in the early evening. Mayb he could talk Leslie into going out to dinner and. . .

Suddenly he remembered that Laurelin had spoken to Lesli on the phone. *What had she said? Had she told Leslie of he relationship with me?* These thoughts haunted him as he gav in to his exhaustion. He'd straighten it all out when he wok up. After all, he had a great deal of confessing to do anyway so he might as well add Laurelin to the list of things to tel Leslie about.

sixteen

When Darrin awoke, he was disoriented and for a moment found it impossible to remember exactly where he was and why. He felt stiff all over and, after stretching, sat up on the edge of the bed to note the time on the clock. The red numerals glared 6:02. *So much for early evening,* he thought. *By the time I get to Lawrence, it'll be at least seven or seven-thirty.*

Getting to his feet, he stretched again and went to pull back the curtains, surprised to note the color of the sky. Something about it just didn't look right. He checked his watch again and then a sudden revelation hit him. He'd slept all night! It wasn't 6:02 on Sunday evening. It was 6:02 Monday morning.

With a groan, he flipped on the television to confirm his suspicions. "Monday morning traffic is backed up on the Shawnee Mission Parkway off of I-35," a female reporter was saying. "Also a non-injury accident at State Line and seventy-fifth is requiring a detour if you're heading north into the city." The male co-anchor joked with her about the road construction detours, which apparently were requiring detours around detours, but Darrin had stopped listening.

Shutting the set off, he sat down on the sofa and ran a hand through his hair. "How could I have slept all night? Leslie will think me a real heel for not at least calling. I promised I'd call on Sunday."

He wondered silently if it was too early to call, then deciding it was, opted for a shower instead. He'd just make up for lost time and no phone call by spending all of Monday with her. And if she couldn't get away from Crossroads, he'd plop down at one of the booths or tables and spend the entire day drinking coffee.

❧

Two hours later, Darrin wheeled the BMW into a parking spot outside of Crossroads and noted the sign in the window. SORRY, WE'RE CLOSED! stared back at him as if putting a physical wall between Darrin and his mission. The trip over had given him a great deal of time to consider how he would break his news to Leslie—not that he hadn't already been considering the hows and whens ever since he'd left for Paris.

He planned first to explain Laurelin. He knew his ex-fiancée well enough to know that she probably made it very clear to Leslie what her status was in his life, at least Laurelin's version of her status. Leslie probably thought him a complete write-off, and he couldn't blame her. He'd made a real mess of things, and only now was he beginning to fear that Leslie would have nothing more to do with him based on the Laurelin issue alone.

Even so, Laurelin's position in his life paled against the reality of his father's position. He'd sent Laurelin packing, but he couldn't just remove the fact that Mike Malone was his father, nor the fact that Mike Malone had killed Leslie's father and mother. That was an issue of such major proportions that Darrin was beginning to feel inadequate to face it.

He sat parked in front of the shop for several minutes before deciding to drive by Leslie's house. If her car was in the drive, he'd stop and visit with her there. If not, he'd head over to the hospital and hope that she'd be able to give him some private time to explain his situation. Either way, Darrin felt more and more apprehensive about facing the truth. He'd come to care about her, love her in a way that he'd never expected. This was the woman he wanted to spend the rest of his life with. Yet, this was also the woman who might never accept him in her life because of the past and what his name would forever be a reminder of.

Slowing down as he drove past the Heyward house, Darrin saw no sign of Leslie's Toyota. *She must be with Travis,* he concluded and headed to the hospital. But, upon entering pediatrics, Kelly greeted him with the same news she'd given him the day before.

"Oh, Darrin, you just missed Leslie. She was here for about half an hour, and she took off. Had some kind of meeting and said she'd be back around lunchtime." She pulled a breakfast tray from a tall, four-wheeled cart and added, "Travis is eating right now, but you're welcome to go on in. He's been moved, you know. It's the third room down that hall." She pointed.

"Thanks, Kelly." Darrin went in search of Travis, hoping that he might shed some light on Leslie's absence.

"Well, hey there, partner. You remember me?" Darrin asked, coming in to find Travis negotiating a bowl of cereal.

"You're Leslie's friend," Travis stated matter-of-factly. "You're Darrin."

"That's right, but I'm your friend, too. At least I'd like to be."

Travis's face lit up, and a smile spread from ear to ear. "Do you like Legos?"

Darrin nodded. "I think they're the best toy in the world."

Travis's face grew contemplative. "They're not just toys."

Darrin realized his mistake instantly. "Oh, of course not." He pulled up a chair alongside the bed. "No, they're really a great deal more than just toys."

Travis nodded as though important information was being shared between two people in the same secret society. "I build things with them," Travis said, dribbling milk down the front of his hospital pajamas as the spoon wobbled on the way to his mouth. "I build a lot."

"I'll bet you do. Have you ever made a whole town out of Legos?" Darrin asked, trying his best to endear himself to the boy.

"Oh, sure," Travis replied. "All the time. The hard thing is to make airplanes and helicopters. I can make them with rubber bands and Legos, and the propellers can really turn."

Darrin smiled in admiration. "That's pretty creative."

"Oh, I saw it in the Lego magazine, but I know a lot of stuff about it already."

Darrin wanted to chuckle at the boy's creative confidence, but instead he decided to change the subject. "Has your sister been in today?"

"Yup," Travis said and turned his concentration on a piece of jellied toast.

"Did she say where she was going? I mean, I know she had some kind of meeting, right?" Darrin asked, hoping the boy wouldn't clam up on him now.

"Sure. She told me," Travis said. His little brows knitted together as he tried to remember. "She was going to the bank for clothes."

"The bank?" Darrin questioned. "She was going to buy clothes at the bank? Maybe she just meant she was going to get some money to buy clothes. Is she going shopping for you—is that who the clothes are for?"

Travis began shaking his head. "No. They're for bears."

Now Darrin was genuinely confused. "For bears? Leslie is buying clothes for bears?"

"That's what she said," Travis replied, seeming completely unconcerned that it made no sense in Darrin's adult world.

"Can you remember exactly what she said, Travis?"

Travis put the toast down as if exasperated with Darrin's inability to understand. "She said she was going to see some bears at the bank for clothes."

Darrin fell silent, trying to make sense of it all, while Travis, seeing that his visitor was apparently satisfied with the answer, continued to eat his breakfast.

Bears? Clothes? What does it mean, God? It just doesn't make any sense. The only thing that did make sense was that Leslie had gone to the bank. Maybe he could catch up with

er there. But which bank and. . .Then a thought came to
Darrin. A very awful thought.

"Travis, are you sure your sister said bears? Could it have
been buyers?"

Travis shrugged. Darrin was feeling a sick dread in the pit
of his stomach. Was Leslie meeting buyers for the shop
because the bank planned to foreclose? Fearing the worse, he
got up. "Travis, I'll be back to see you later. Can I bring you
anything?"

Travis beamed a smiled. "There's a new Lego set with
enough stuff to build a time machine," he said in an offhand
manner. "You could bring that."

"You got it, buddy. If I can find it, it's yours."

With that Darrin fairly flew out of the hospital, pausing
only long enough to call Leslie's house. With any luck at all,
he'd get ahold of Leslie's aunt Margie and perhaps she would
be able to tell him where Leslie had gone. If Leslie was planning to sell the shop because the bank was threatening fore-
closure, he had to stop her.

Filling Margie in on the details, including the fact that he'd
already arranged to pay Travis's hospital bill, Darrin was
finally given the information he needed to stop Leslie from
selling Crossroads. He arrived at the bank, and after insisting
the receptionist interrupt the meeting, practically dragged
Leslie into the hall outside the office.

Her stunned expression did little to calm his nerves. "Look,
you need to stop what you're doing and come with me."

"Why? Is something wrong with Travis?" Leslie asked,
looking suddenly panicked.

"No," Darrin assured her, "but you don't have to do this. I
can't explain it all here, but put your people off. Tell them
you've changed your mind, or that I made you a better deal,
or whatever, but just put an end to this meeting and come
back to Crossroads with me."

"Darrin, I'm in the middle of—"

"I know what you're in the middle of, and you don't have to sell the shop. Just come with me, and I'll explain." Darrin persisted.

"All right, Darrin," Leslie said, exasperation edging her voice, "but this better be good."

❧

Back at Crossroads, Leslie allowed Darrin to take charge and lead her to the table in the very back of the shop. He sat down opposite her, seeing the confusion written in her expression, and sighed.

"This isn't going to be easy for me, Leslie, but I have a great deal I need to tell you."

"Like about your fiancée?" Leslie asked, her blue-green eyes searching for the truth in his face.

"Ex-fiancée," he stated clearly. Then changing his mind as to the order in which he would confess his sins, Darrin continued. "Yes, I want to explain about her as well, but first and foremost, I feel I have to tell you something of much greater importance."

"All right," Leslie replied, sounding much calmer than she looked.

Darrin sighed again. *Where do I begin?* he wondered. "You don't need to worry about the shop," he finally said. "First of all, if there is a problem with the rent or the bills or whatever, I want you to know that I intend to see it taken care of."

"But—"

"No, hear me out," Darrin said, halting her questions. "I've already arranged to pay for Travis's hospital bills, and if your time away from Crossroads has caused problems with the bank, then I'll take care of that as well."

Leslie's mouth dropped open in surprise. "But, Darrin," she insisted, "Travis's bill is going to amount to more than fifteen thousand dollars. I can't let you pay that. You don't even know us, and we certainly don't know you. There's absolutely nothing to connect you to us, and certainly nothing to obligate you to seeing to our welfare."

Darrin frowned. "But there is, Leslie. You see," he paused trying to find just the right words, "what I'm going to tell you will probably change things between us forever, but I just want to tell you something first, before I explain any more about why I'm doing this. I've fallen in love with you."

The color drained from her face, and she sat back hard against the chair.

"I told you that I wanted to be more than friends, and I meant it. I meant it because I've lost my heart to you and. . ." He stopped. "This isn't what I came here to say."

"Then what?" Leslie managed to ask.

Darrin stood and paced the aisle between the table and the counter. "Leslie, my name is Darrin Malone. I live in Kansas City, and the first time I ever set eyes on you was on our flight down to Dallas."

"You were the man next to me. I remember you now," Leslie said, gasping in surprise. "I thought you looked familiar, but I could never place it. Of course, I had a lot on my mind then."

"I know," Darrin replied. "The thing is, we share a great deal and most of it you aren't even aware of, but when you understand the full details, you may never speak to me again. I'm just begging you to hear me out before you try to throw me out."

"Why would I throw you out?" Leslie asked, shaking her head in confusion.

"Because I'm Darrin Malone."

"But that doesn't mean anything to—" She stopped in mid-sentence. "Malone?"

"Yes," Darrin said, nodding. "I'm Darrin Malone, and my father is, or rather was, Michael Malone—the man responsible for killing your parents."

seventeen

"Darrin, how? I mean, why didn't you. . ." Leslie shook her head in disbelief. This couldn't be real. He couldn't be telling her that he was part of her pain. "Your father was the man who. . ." She couldn't bring herself to say the rest.

She watched through tears that threatened to spill over as Darrin began to pace nervously. Shoving his hands deep into his pockets, he struggled to continue. "I don't really know how to explain all this to you, Leslie. You see, my father and I were never close. He had always been an alcoholic, for as long as I could remember. He and my mother separated, and after she died from cancer, I was his only living relative. I grew up hating him for killing my mother through his drunken acts of stupidity, making her a nervous wreck. He was always getting into wrecks and fender-benders, but this was the first time anyone was ever injured by his carelessness, besides himself.

"I was the one the Dallas police department located to identify his body and make arrangements for burial and so on. I met you on the plane ride down, and I think you've had my heart ever since. It wasn't until later that night when the story was on the evening news that I finally figured out who you really were and who the victims of my father's foolishness were. I was overwhelmed by guilt and anger. I felt I had to make things right, no matter the cost. I found out all I could about you and your remaining family, and that's how I came to Crossroads and to you."

He paused, and Leslie could tell he was monitoring her for some response, but she was unable to say anything. The reality of Darrin's role seeped into her consciousness. She sat completely motionless and waited for him to continue.

"Then, Travis got sick, and I insisted that all his bills be sent to me. I instructed it to be done in secret because I knew you would never accept my help outright. I meant to tell you before you found out the total, but obviously, I was a little late. That's why you don't have to sell the shop."

Leslie felt tears hot on her cheeks. "So you did all this out of guilt? You never really cared for me or for Travis? Do you even *like* raspberry lattes?" She knew it sounded insignificant, but she had to know if it was a farce—if everything he had done had been to absolve his conscience.

Darrin sat down at the table. "No, no, Leslie. I do care about you and Travis and Crossroads. That's what I need you to see. It began as guilt, but I came to care about you beyond that. I would've helped you even if I hadn't known about—"

"No, you wouldn't have! I never would have met you if you hadn't been racked with guilt. You would never have come back into my life. And that really scares me. I've come to care about you quite a bit, Darrin, and I truly thought of you as a friend. I still do. I just wish you had told me the truth from the beginning."

Leslie couldn't tell what she was feeling. It was like rage, disappointment, frustration, and hurt all wrapped up into one. She loved this man. She really did. Not for the reasons she thought she would fall in love when she was a teenager, but for so much more. For the way his patience never ran out with her. For the way he would sit with her for hours on end in a hospital waiting room. For talking with her and allowing her to vent her frustrations, her worries, and her troubles. For smiling that Darrin-smile whenever he spotted her in the coffee shop. Now, she realized that the man she had lost her heart to was the son of the drunk driver who had killed her parents. This fact was supposed to change everything, at least in Darrin's eyes. But did it?

"Leslie, I need to know what you're feeling."

"How can I tell you what I'm feeling when I don't even know what it is, myself?"

"I understand, but I need to know where I stand with you." His eyes were pleading, and his face was strained with compassion.

"It's not your job to look out for me or to repair the damage he did. But. . ." Leslie stopped and sighed.

"But what?"

"I can't accept your help. It's not right. I don't want to be obligated to you. . ."

"Leslie, didn't you pray for help? Didn't you ask God to help you and protect you through this time of trial?" Leslie nodded. "Why can't I be that help? Why can't I be the one God sent to help you through this?"

"No!" she said adamantly. "I don't want to be tied any closer to you than I already am!" She looked away, as though ashamed of the implication of her feelings. Her long blond hair fell over her shoulders and framed her face. Bringing her gaze back to meet his, she watched as pain crept into his eyes.

"Leslie, talk to me. Don't hide your feelings from me. Not now. This is too important." His dark blue eyes implored her to open up. "I need to know you don't hate me. At least that. If you don't love me, fine. I just can't stand to think you despise me."

Leslie immediately felt guilt for the harshness of her words. She hated to hurt anyone. "It just wouldn't be appropriate." Her expression softened. "I can't lie to you, Darrin. Despite all my willpower and all my determination, I fell in love with you, too. But it doesn't matter what I feel for you. You have a fiancée," she offered weakly.

"Ex-fiancée. Leslie, that's over. It was over a long time ago, at least to anyone astute enough to see the warning signs. Laurelin and I were never right for each other. When you called, I was just about to explain to Laurelin that I was breaking off the engagement. Ever since the accident, God has been working me over in a major way. I came to realize that Lin and I didn't share the same faith or the same values or even the same interests. She had a way of making herself convenient, and I was desperate enough to fall into her trap. When I listened to my heart and sought God's way, instead of Darrin Malone's way, I was led to the truth. The Lord led me away from Laurelin, and He led me to you."

Leslie shook her head in exasperation. "Darrin, I don't know what to think. I don't know why you're here, and I don't know how to feel about you or about us. You said you loved me, but then you tell me that guilt and shame brought you into my life. How can we build a relationship off that?"

"We already have, but there's so much more, Leslie. I do love you. And not because I feel obligated to. I fell in love with the woman I saw day after day. The woman who struggled but managed to keep on going. The woman who confided her fears to me and who laughed with me. The woman who was not afraid to be honest and up front with me, even though she had no real idea who I was. I love you, Leslie. I hope that you can forgive me for not telling you the truth about my father and about my presence in your life. I was just so afraid you would hate me for who I was."

"What kind of person do you think I am? How could anyone blame you because of your father's deeds? You didn't hand him the drinks or the keys. You didn't demand that he drive that night or encourage him to hit my parents' car. You had nothing to do with it. I do love you. But not because you were saving me from the evils of this world. It was because you were sharing them with me. I don't want a savior, Darrin. I have one, and His name is Jesus. I don't expect you to right the wrongs of my life. That's not what I need." She placed a hand over Darrin's. "I need you to be my friend and my companion. I need you to be more. But you can't be of any good to either of us if you're trying to atone for the sins of your father. You have to let that go, and you have to forgive him. It took a lot of prayer and a lot of God's grace to allow me to forgive your father, but I did. You need to do the same."

Darrin's eyes filled with tears. "It's so hard. I try. I really do. I just thought that you'd hate me if you knew the truth. I felt so bad that he'd taken them away from you. I wanted to help you, but I didn't want you to think I was being some great martyr. The more I was with you, the more I came to love you and admire you for your strength and your faith. Even now, you still amaze me with your confidence and your trust. I can't say that I never doubted God or that in your position I would even be able to maintain my faith."

Leslie smiled sympathetically. "I know what you mean. I wish you could've heard me during the days following the accident. I was so lost. I blamed God. I blamed your father. I blamed everything. Margie helped me deal with my anger and brought me back to the truth. I can't say I did it all on my own. And I'm not saying you have to do it all on your own, either."

Darrin sat, looking deep into her eyes. "Are you saying. . ."

"Yes, Darrin, I still love you. I want to help you through your pain and your guilt. But I need to know that you didn't just befriend me because of your guilty conscience."

For the first time that evening, Leslie saw a smile play at his lips. "No, no, Ms. Heyward. I have a great many other reasons for befriending you."

Leslie was glad to feel the weight of the conversation lighten considerably. She allowed herself to counter his playful grin with one of her own. "And, pray tell, Mr. Malone, what are these great many reasons you speak of?"

"Well, Ms. Heyward, I love you and fully intend to make you my bride."

The weight was immediately back in place, and Leslie felt

as though he had knocked the wind from her. "Marriage? You're talking marriage? Oh, Darrin, I need to think. . .to pray. . .to—"

"To hush." He rose to his feet and held out his arms to her. She took hold of his hand and stood as well. He encircled her with his broad arms and turned his eyes down to meet hers. Gently, he kissed her, and Leslie felt all her cares melt away. When he drew away, she wanted to pull him back, but she refrained.

"Now, Ms. Heyward, that seems to have quieted you for a bit. I think I will take you home now and allow you to consider the prospect of being my wife."

Leslie nodded, wondering if her legs would support her all the way out to the car. Why had he chosen a table so far back? "That would probably be best, Mr. Malone."

eighteen

Leslie spent the rest of the day praying about Darrin and the proposal. She told Margie that there were major decisions to be made and that she needed to pray in private. Margie understood and offered to go to the hospital and keep Travis company, while Leslie secluded herself.

Leslie was grateful for Margie's love and understanding. She had always been able to count on her aunt, and this time was no exception. Even when she heard Margie return that evening, Leslie remained in her room, fasting and praying that she might seek only God's will. It would be easy to taint her actions by relying on emotions, and Leslie was determined that this wouldn't be the case.

Yet even as she sent her prayers heavenward, she knew a peace and rightness about it that gave her confidence. She loved Darrin, and for the first time in her life, she knew what it was to desire to spend the rest of her life with a man.

The next morning, Leslie knew it was time to confide in Margie. She had been so closed-mouth on the situation that no doubt Margie had stewed and fretted throughout the night. She had just finished putting breakfast together when a sleepy-eyed Margie entered the kitchen. "Good morning," Leslie called cheerily.

"Well, something certainly seems to agree with you," Margie said, stifling a yawn. "I take it you worked through your problems."

"That and more. Aunt Margie, we need to talk," Leslie said, pulling out a chair for her aunt. "I have breakfast on the table and thought we might share it and discuss the future."

162

"The future?"

"Exactly," Leslie said with a grin.

After they prayed, Margie looked up at Leslie with hopeful expectation. She said nothing, but Leslie could tell she wanted to.

"I have a great deal to confide in you. The first thing is that Darrin has already seen to paying off Travis's hospital bill, and he wants to help us keep the shop." Margie said nothing, and Leslie continued. "Secondly, Darrin and I are in love, and he has asked me to marry him."

"Are you serious? When did this happen?"

Leslie picked up a piece of bacon and nibbled at it. "I'm very serious, and I suppose I should start back at the beginning. It all started when I went to Dallas. . ."

Leslie told Margie everything, and when she was finished, she sat back and offered one single question. "Can you forgive Darrin's connection to Mom and Dad's death?"

Margie's brows knit together, and her face contorted into several looks before settling on a stern, authoritative expression. "That young man has nothing to be forgiven of," she said sternly.

"Oh, but he feels he does," Leslie replied. "He feels like he should have been able to do something before it all came to this. I have to admit, when he first told me, I wasn't too inclined to remain in the same room with him. Not because I blamed him, but because I kept thinking, 'This is the son of the man who killed my parents.' "

"You obviously don't feel that way now," Margie replied.

"No, I don't. I've prayed through every aspect of this situation, and while I will forever mourn the premature passing of my parents, I know that Darrin had nothing but goodness in his heart when he came to us. He didn't want to deceive us, but he knew we wouldn't take well to his offering help when the hurt was so raw and fresh. And Margie, he was right to do it the way he did. I'd have never given him the time of day if he'd walked into Crossroads and announced that he was Michael Malone's son."

"But neither would you have held him responsible for what happened. I know you too well to believe otherwise."

"You're right, but I wouldn't have wanted to associate with him. I would have politely accepted his apology, told him we absolved him of any responsibility, and bye-bye, Mr. Malone."

"So, you're going to marry him?"

"Would that bother you?" Leslie asked quite seriously.

Margie's face lit up in a grin. "Bother me? It'll only bother me if you don't allow me to help plan the wedding. Darrin's too good to let get away, and if you don't snatch him up, some more fortunate woman will."

Leslie beamed. "I'm glad you feel that way, because I intend to reel Mr. Malone in, hook, line, and sinker."

"And maybe in doing so, the past will be laid to rest once and for all," Margie commented. "Maybe Darrin will finally realize that you love him more than the memories he might invoke, memories that relate to his father."

"I hope so, Margie," Leslie said. "I hope so."

❧

At the hospital, Leslie found Travis intent on the Lego time machine Darrin had brought him. "Hey, buddy," she said, coming into the room, "the doctor tells me that you can go home tomorrow."

"Shhh," Travis said, without so much as looking up. "This is a real hard part, and I have to. . .Ahhh!" he exclaimed in disgust as a big piece broke away from the others. "Break, break, break. It always has to break."

Leslie put her hand to the small boy's shoulder. "Trav, stop acting that way. Just rest for a minute and listen to me tell you something else. Then, after you've rested, you'll probably be able to make it work the very first time you try."

Travis didn't appear to believe her, but nevertheless he waited. "Tell me what?"

Leslie smiled. "I know you don't know Darrin very well—"

"I like Darrin. He brought me these Legos and some books, and he talked to me," Travis interrupted.

Leslie smiled. "I'm glad you like him, because I like him a lot, too. In fact, I love him, and he wants to marry me."

"Marry? Like Mommy and Daddy were married?" Travis asked, suddenly frowning.

"That's right. What would you think of that?" Leslie was stunned when Travis's face puckered into a tearful expression. "What's wrong, Trav?"

"Where will I go live when you go away with him?" Travis asked, trying hard not to cry.

"Oh, baby, I would never go live anywhere without you. You're part of the package." But suddenly it dawned on her that maybe Darrin didn't realize this. What if Darrin presumed that Margie would take Travis?

"I'd get to live with you and Darrin?" Travis asked, all traces of his frown disappearing.

"Of course," Leslie muttered, still contemplating the situation. Why hadn't she thought to talk to Darrin about all of this first? She shook the discouraging thoughts away. "Travis, believe me, I would never ask you to live with anyone who didn't love you as much as I do. Will you trust me on this one?"

"Okay."

She embraced him in a tight squeeze, then tousled his hair and kissed his cheek. "I love you, Travis. You will always be my sweet baby guy."

He smiled at her, then seemed to forget the crisis of a few moments earlier and began to take up his Lego work again. "I've got to build this before Darrin comes to see me."

Leslie nodded. *And I have to talk to Darrin before he comes up here,* she thought.

❧

A call placed from Leslie to Darrin sent him to the Heyward house, where she was waiting for him. "I'm sorry if I interrupted something important," Leslie said, meeting him on the porch, "but I have something we should discuss."

The gravity of her tone made him wince. "Am I not going to like this discussion?"

Leslie smiled. "I suppose it all depends."

"On what?"

"On whether you kiss me hello and come sit with me on the porch and enjoy the sunshine of this glorious day."

He grinned. "I suppose I can bear that." He wrapped her in his arms and sighed against her ear before kissing her cheek, then her nose, then each of her eyes, and finally her mouth. "How's that for a hello?" he asked with a mischievous twinkle in his eye.

"Ummm," she said and put her head against his shoulder. "Hello. Hello. Hello," she murmured.

"So does this mean you have good news for me?" Darrin asked, pulling away to catch the dreamy expression on her face before she covered it with a more sober one.

"I want to have good news for you, but we need to cover a few bases first."

Darrin's grin broadened. "I've heard about making it to different bases, I just never thought—"

Leslie elbowed his ribs and pushed away. "Now, Darrin Malone, you know very well that that's *not* the kind of bases I'm talking about. Come on and sit down with me."

He followed her to a set of wicker porch chairs and waited until she'd chosen the settee before motioning her to scoot over and allow him to sit beside her. Leslie did as he wanted but held up her hand.

"I brought you hear to talk, not neck."

"Can't we do both?"

She laughed, and it seemed to lighten the moment. "Maybe later. But first, you listen."

"Okay, I'm all ears." Darrin leaned back and held his breath. *What could she possibly need to cover that required a special meeting like this?*

"First of all, I've given the whole matter of us over to God. I prayed and fasted and felt very confident in the answers and peace that came because of those prayers."

"But?" Darrin said, finally daring to exhale.

Leslie's expression softened and her blue-green eyes sought his with great love. "As far am I'm concerned there are no buts, however you may feel differently once I explain."

"I doubt that quite seriously, but please explain so we can move on to second base," he said with a roguish grin.

"Now stop that. This really is very serious." Her tone told him that she was exasperated with his teasing.

"Okay, Les, tell me what has you so troubled and worried."

She folded her hands and stared at her fingers for a moment. Darrin longed to reach out and brush back the blond hair that had fallen forward across her shoulder, but instead he sat back and remained silent. Whatever she wanted to say, he needed to let her know he understood the importance of the moment.

"Darrin, I went to tell Travis about us, and he started to cry," she said, then paused to look up. "He wanted to know where he'd have to go when we got married and went away."

Darrin suddenly understood Leslie's apprehension. They'd never discussed the boy, but Darrin thought it was a given— that he and Leslie would raise him. "And what did you say?" he asked softly.

Leslie bit at her lower lip and then let out a tremendous sigh. "I told him that I loved him, and that I would never ask him to live with someone who didn't love him as much as I did."

Darrin took hold of her hand. "Then it should work out just fine, because I do love him, and I wouldn't tolerate you sending him anywhere else."

Leslie's eyes widened. "You mean it? After all, this is a big deal. Raising a child isn't going to be easy."

"Never figured it would be, but I like the idea of having a great many of our own, so Travis can just start us out in style, and we'll practice on him until we get it right. Then he can play big brother to the others."

Leslie fell into Darrin's arms. "I love you so much. I just knew this was how you'd feel."

"Then why did you become so scared a minute ago?" he asked, gently stroking her arm with his finger.

"I guess because I wanted this so much. I want to marry you. I want us to be a family. Oh, Darrin, I just want you."

He chuckled and felt a warmth of satisfaction spread through him like a wash of pride. *She doesn't care about the past,* he thought. *She cares more about the future than anything laying back there.* It was exactly what he had hoped for. Prayed for.

"And I want you—and I want Travis, too," he finally said and pulled her even tighter against him. "For all time—no matter what."

"I felt like I was standing at a crossroad," Leslie whispered, placing her hand atop his arm. "One way led me down a dark and lonely path."

"And the other?"

She pulled away and turned to see his face. Her hand reached up to touch his cheek. "The other led me to you."

epilogue

"Flight attendants prepare the cabin for landing," the voice of the airline captain sounded over the intercom.

Leslie rechecked her seat belt and looked up to find a nicely tanned Darrin smiling at her. "What?" she asked, glancing back down at her Hawaiian print blouse. "Did I spill something?"

"No, not that anyone could notice against *that* wild print," he said grinning. "I was just thinking of how much I love you and how happy I am that you're my wife."

"And I am very happy to be your wife, Mr. Malone. Hawaii seems to have agreed with you. You should take honeymoons more often."

"Perhaps I will," he said, leaning close, "but only if you're included in the trip."

"But of course," she replied and reached over to squeeze his hand. "I'm afraid you're stuck with me."

"When I'm afraid," Darrin quoted the Psalmist, "I will trust in You." He looked heavenward. "There's not much we can't face if we put God at the helm, eh?"

"You're right," Leslie agreed. "I'm so excited about seeing Travis. I hope he likes his birthday present. Margie said she has the party all set up for us to celebrate when we get home. It's going to be such a surprise for him."

"Six years old and in two weeks, school starts," Darrin replied. "He's got a busy year ahead of him."

"So do we," Leslie said, glancing out the window as the plane finally touched ground. She sighed. It was good to be home.

Darrin interlaced his fingers with hers. "We can handle it. So long as we work together. Remember what the counselor said? Every family has to work together as a unit. Doesn't matter if it's a blended family or one that comes together under the loving union of one man and woman. We'll work together. Even Travis recognizes that."

"Yeah, especially after the counselor used Legos to make his point," Leslie laughed.

The flight attendant announced their arrival, and the minute the seat belt sign was turned off, Leslie jumped to her feet and motioned Darrin into the aisle. "Hurry," she said. "We don't want to keep him waiting!"

They grabbed up their carry-on bags and moved out of the plane and up the terminal ramp. Leslie could scarcely contain herself and ran the final ten or fifteen feet, edging around other people and prying herself through a narrow opening where an empty wheelchair blocked one side of the hall and a backpacking youth sauntered up the other side.

Then she saw him standing beside Margie. The look of expectation causing his eyes to be wide and searching.

"Travis!" she squealed and practically flew out of the security area to where her little brother waited. "Travis!"

She picked him up and whirled around to catch the loving expression of her husband. It was still so amazing to see how God had turned the sad and tragic death of her parents into something so positive and right.

Margie laughed and greeted Darrin. "Good to have you back. How was your flight?"

Leslie didn't hear her husband's answer because Travis had wrapped his arms around her and was squeezing her neck in a bearlike grip. "Now, we're a real family, aren't we, Sissy?"

She looked up to see that Darrin, too, had heard the question. His nod reassured her. "You bet we are, Travis. You and me and Darrin, and Aunt Margie, too. We're a family, and together with God, there isn't anything we can't face."

And in her heart, she knew it was true. Life would be filled with crossroads, but with God leading the way, the path would always be certain—the choice would always be right.

A Letter To Our Readers

Dear Reader:

In order that we might better contribute to your reading enjoyment, we would appreciate your taking a few minutes to respond to the following questions. When completed, please return to the following:

Rebecca Germany, Managing Editor
Heartsong Presents
P.O. Box 719
Uhrichsville, Ohio 44683

. Did you enjoy reading *Crossroads?*
   ☐ Very much. I would like to see more books
      by this author!
   ☐ Moderately
      I would have enjoyed it more if _____

   _____

Are you a member of **Heartsong Presents**? ☐Yes ☐No
If no, where did you purchase this book?_____

_____

What influenced your decision to purchase this
book? (Check those that apply.)

   ☐ Cover   ☐ Back cover copy

   ☐ Title   ☐ Friends

   ☐ Publicity   ☐ Other_____

How would you rate, on a scale from 1 (poor) to 5
(superior), the cover design?_____

5. On a scale from 1 (poor) to 10 (superior), please rate
    the following elements.

    ___Heroine   ___Plot

    ___Hero   ___Inspirational theme

    ___Setting   ___Secondary characters

6. What settings would you like to see covered in
    Heartsong Presents books?_____
    _____
    _____

7. What are some inspirational themes you would like
    to see treated in future books?_____
    _____
    _____

8. Would you be interested in reading other **Heartsong
    Presents** titles?   ❏ Yes   ❏ No

9. Please check your age range:
    ❏ Under 18   ❏ 18-24   ❏ 25-34
    ❏ 35-45   ❏ 46-55   ❏ Over 55

10. How many hours per week do you read? _____

Name _____

Occupation_____

Address_____

City_____ State_____ Zip _____